the BACKWARD Season

a Wishing Day Novel

ALSO BY LAUREN MYRACLE

Ten

Eleven

Twelve

Thirteen

Thirteen Plus One

The Fashion Disaster That Changed My Life

The Flower Power series

ttyl

ttfn

l8r, g8r

yolo

Peace, Love, and Baby Ducks

Shine

Kissing Kate

The Infinite Moment of Us

Wishing Day

The Forgetting Spell

LAUREN MYRACLE

the
BACKWARD
Season

a
Wishing Day
Novel

 KATHERINE TEGEN BOOKS
An Imprint of HarperCollins Publishers

Katherine Tegen Books is an imprint of HarperCollins Publishers.

The Backward Season

Library of Congress Control Number: 2017943403
ISBN 978-0-06-234212-6

Typography by Carla Weise
18 19 20 21 22 CG/LSCH 10 9 8 7 6 5 4 3 2 1
❖
First Edition

*For Ellen Evangelista
and Kate Zaparaniuk*

I wish for the thing with feathers
that perches in the soul
and sings the tune without the words
and never stops at all.

—KLARA BLOK, AGE THIRTY-SIX

CHAPTER ONE

Ava

"My Wishing Day is in *two days*," Ava said. Somehow, incomprehensibly, her sisters seemed oblivious to the urgency of the situation. That's why she'd called this emergency powwow under the ancient willow tree—only they *still* weren't taking it seriously. "We have to figure out what I should wish for. I'm our last hope!"

"Our last hope?" Darya said. "Like Obi-Wan Kenobi?" She leaned over and rubbed the top of Ava's head with her knuckles. "You are so cute."

Ava ducked free. "I'm not cute. Stop saying that!"

"Natasha, we're not allowed to tell Ava she's cute

anymore." Darya held up her hands, palms out. "Her words, not mine."

Natasha half smiled. "But you *are* cute, Ava. You're adorable, inside and out."

Ava wanted to thwack her palm against her forehead. Labels like "cute" and "adorable" drove her up the wall. They were so . . . small. There was no way a handful of adjectives could sum up Ava's essence.

The same held true for her sisters. Fourteen-year-old Natasha, for example, was usually described as pretty, with thick, dark hair like Mama's. But she was so much more than "pretty." She was solemn, bookish, and compassionate. She believed in fairness. She wanted to make the world a better place. Didn't those qualities matter more than what Natasha looked like?

Darya was the middle sister, five and a half months older than Ava and ten months younger than Natasha. If Ava was cute and Natasha pretty, then Darya—it had to be said—was stunning. Her auburn curls tumbled down her back, a torrent of liquid gold. People stopped her on the street and asked if they could touch it—for real. Darya rolled her eyes, but only for show. In truth, Darya lapped up the attention.

Darya was also impatient, opinionated, and prickly,

especially if things didn't go her way. And she was funny, and she was loyal, and she cared about things far more than she let on.

Ava struggled to untangle her thoughts, which flew all over the place when she grappled with the question of identity. Like why were girls, especially, judged on how they looked?

When Ava was younger, things were simpler. If someone had asked her who she was, she'd have said, "Um, I'm *Ava*," and she'd have given the person a funny look.

Now that she was older, Ava wondered if *anybody* knew who they were, really and truly. Yes, Ava was Ava. Yes, she was probably cute, as Darya and Natasha insisted. To them, she was the cute sister, the dreamy sister, the baby sister.

But surely she was more than that. She had to be, because her family was broken, and she was the only person left to set things right. She leaned against the rough bark of the willow tree and sighed. She looked pointedly at her journal, whose pages she'd planned to fill with Natasha's and Darya's advice. It remained closed on her lap, its pages blank. She sighed again.

"Omigosh, enough with the sighing," Darya said.

"Then help me!" Ava pleaded. "Don't you want

our family to be whole again?"

"Our family *is* whole again," Darya said. "Mama came back. She's not missing anymore."

Ava dragged her hand over her face. "Mama is back in Willow Hill, yes. But come on. She's been hiding out in Aunt Elena's apartment for *over a year*. No one knows except Aunt Elena and the three of us. Not even Papa!"

"So?" Darya said. "She isn't *gone* anymore. That's what matters. She returned from . . . well, wherever she was all those years. And for that, we have Natasha to thank." Darya dipped her head at Natasha. "Thank you, Natasha."

"You're welcome?" said Natasha.

"*And*, Natasha didn't force us into a group huddle before her Wishing Day," Darya continued. "She made her Wishing Day wishes and moved on."

"I don't understand how you're okay with this," Ava said.

"I'll tell you how. Because thanks to one of *my* Wishing Day wishes, Mama *is* going to tell Papa that she's back," Darya said. For just a moment, she faltered. "She promised."

"She made that promise in October," Ava protested. "It's the middle of May, Darya. It's been over half a year."

Darya fluttered her fingers.

"Plus, Angela's been added to the picture, also thanks to you," Ava said. "I'm not saying that to make you feel bad, but it's true."

"I wished for Papa to be happy again, and he is. So sue me."

"Happy?" asked Natasha. "Happi*er*, maybe. But that wouldn't take much."

The three sisters fell silent, because when Mama disappeared so many years ago, Papa disappeared, too. No, he hadn't abandoned them the way Mama had. He had probably even done his best to handle what had been thrown at him. Just, his best wasn't all that great.

"For the record, I never intended for Papa to meet a hippie-chick jewelry maker at one of those craft fairs his life revolves around," Darya grumbled. "She doesn't even make good jewelry. Couldn't she at least make *good* jewelry?"

"I like Angela," Natasha said. She regarded the cuff bracelet circling her slender wrist. "I like her jewelry, too. That doesn't mean I want her to be Papa's girlfriend."

Ava gathered her courage. "Mama hiding out at Aunt Elena's is bad," she said. "Angela hanging around Papa is also bad." She tilted her head and studied

5

the maze of leaves and branches above her. So many interwoven strands. Reluctantly, she brought her gaze down. "But the real problem is Emily."

Darya's jaw tightened.

Natasha pressed her fingers to her temples. "Ava, that's a nonstarter."

"A 'nonstarter'?" Ava said. "I think it's the opposite of a nonstarter. What happened to Emily started it all."

"Mama needs to let go of Emily," Darya said.

"How?" Ava asked. "Emily was Mama's best friend." She appealed to Natasha. "*You* understand. You're the one who learned about Emily in the first place."

Natasha shook her head. "Trust me, Ava, I've gone around and around about the Emily thing."

"The Emily thing?!"

"But what do we really know? At the end of the day, all we have is Mama's word."

"So?" Ava said. "When *you* tell *me* something, I believe you. When you told me about Emily, I believed you. I still do!"

"Ava," said Natasha, and there it was in her tone again. Little Ava, cute Ava, gullible Ava. The baby of the family, too young for grown-up problems. "What if Mama made Emily up? What if she invented her, like an imaginary friend?"

Tears pricked Ava's eyes. *Like an imaginary friend?!* For heaven's sake, Ava was thirteen, not three.

"I realize it's confusing," Natasha said gently. "But it's a possibility we have to consider."

"Not me. I know Emily was real."

"Except you don't!" Darya said.

Ava fought her frustration. Darya wasn't pretty when she was exasperated. Her teeth looked too little, her lips too twitchy.

"According to Mama, Emily was Papa's little sister," Darya said. "So why doesn't Papa have any recollection of her existence?" She narrowed her eyes. "Little sisters are generally hard to forget."

"The Bird Lady said Emily existed," Ava said stubbornly.

"The Bird Lady?" Darya exclaimed. "You think *she's* a reliable source?"

"I thought you liked the Bird Lady!" said Ava.

Spots of red bloomed on Darya's cheeks. "I do. I'm just . . . all I'm saying . . ." She clamped her twitching lips shut.

Ava considered what she knew about the Bird Lady, which wasn't much. She was as old as a mountain and as wrinkled as a prune, and the reason everyone called her the Bird Lady was because wherever she went, birds followed. Sometimes they perched on her shoulder. Sometimes they nestled in the thick white tangle of her hair. If she was wearing a hat, they rode jauntily on its brim.

Ava didn't know what the Bird Lady's real name was, she realized.

Did anyone?

"The Bird Lady mentioned Emily to both of you around the time of your Wishing Days," Ava said. Her eyes met Natasha's first, and then Darya's. "Are you sticking to that part of the story, or are you taking it back as well?"

"The Bird Lady did tell me about Emily," Natasha admitted. "But I'm with Darya. I'm not sure how much we can trust her."

"Why?"

Natasha stretched out her legs, and the willow's fronds rustled, making the sun cast dancing shadows on her shins. Ava thought Natasha was going to dodge the question, but Natasha said, "I asked her to leave me alone, but she wouldn't. She disguised herself as a school cafeteria lady to trick me into talking to her."

"What?" Ava said.

"She stole one of the school's serving spoons. She wore a fake mole."

"A fake *mole*?" Ava echoed.

Darya snorted. "When she tracked me down, she was wearing an enormous sombrero with felt balls dangling from the rim."

Fake moles, felt balls . . .

"But she said that Emily was real," Ava insisted. "She said that to both of you."

"What if she was lying?" Darya said. "Or *fibbing*. The Bird Lady is more of a fibber than a liar, I think."

"Meaning what?"

Natasha drummed her fingers on her thigh. "She doled out information in half-truths," she said, and Darya nodded. "She was . . . cagey. I always had the sense she was hiding something."

"Me too!" said Darya. "At one point, I asked her flat out what she wasn't telling me, but she clammed up and did one of her disappearing acts."

"Her disappearing acts," Natasha repeated wryly. "Another example of why she's not the best source." She cocked her head. "Darya, did you ever get the sense that she *wanted* to say more, but for some reason she couldn't?"

Darya's eyes shifted. She gnawed on her thumbnail.

"Did *you* get that sense, Natasha?" Ava asked. "You must have, or you wouldn't have asked." She knew she was onto something, because a new emotion charged the air. "You said 'couldn't.' You said you got the feeling that the Bird Lady *wanted* to say more, but *couldn't*. What would keep her from saying something she wanted to say?"

Natasha put her hand on her collarbone, a gesture Ava knew. It meant Natasha was nervous.

"Do you think she made a promise to someone?" Ava pressed. "And, like, she couldn't break that person's trust?"

Natasha shrugged.

Darya held herself still, looking fixedly at nothing.

"Omigosh," Ava exclaimed. A pure white space opened inside of her, and she knew. She knew what her sisters thought, but weren't allowing themselves to say. "You think someone put a curse on her!"

Neither Natasha nor Darya contradicted her. Neither even flinched at her use of what most would consider a "babyish" concept: a curse. And not a symbolic curse, but a literal one.

"If someone put a curse on her, that means magic was involved. If magic was involved, then it *had* to do with Mama and Emily!"

Natasha blushed.

"You're making connections out of thin air," Darya said. "Also? Curses only exist in fairy tales."

"*Riiiiight,*" Ava said. "Whereas magic and wishes and Wishing Days, on the other hand . . ."

"What if the Bird Lady's nuts?" Natasha said in a rush. "Not just kooky, but diagnostically crazy?"

Darya pursed her lips. "Like Papa's mom's mom? The one with the weird name?"

"Elnora," said Natasha.

"Great-Grandma Elnora wasn't crazy," Ava said indignantly. "She was eccentric, and because of that, she and Grandma Rose had a rocky relationship. That's what Papa said. Like, Great-Grandma Elnora never hid the fact that she believed in magic, and as we all know, Grandma Rose—"

Ava broke off. "Grandma Rose! Holy fudge nuggets!"

"What?" Darya said.

Ava raced to put her thoughts in order. Papa's mother, Grandma Rose, lived in a nursing home. Grandma Rose was the only grandparent the girls had a relationship with, because Mama's parents had died before the girls were born, and Papa's father wasn't

11

really in the picture. He and Grandma Rose got divorced when Papa was a teenager. He lived in California, and his name was Dave. Grandpa Dave, who she and Natasha and Darya had never met.

Darya snapped her fingers in front of Ava's face. "Ava. Why the holy fudge nuggets?"

"Because Grandma Rose, who is Great-Grandma Elnora's daughter, *believes in Emily*," Ava marveled. "Want to know how I know? Because she called me Emily once!"

Natasha crinkled her forehead.

"And you can't write off Grandma Rose as being kooky or nuts or eccentric, at least not in the 'believing in magic and curses and stuff' way," Ava said, her words tumbling over one another. "Grandma Rose rejects all of that stuff. Think about it: What's Papa's one rule for when we visit her?"

"That we don't bring up magic," Darya said grudgingly.

"Because she's *not* a believer," Natasha added.

Ava's pulse fluttered. "But she called me Emily. At the nursing home, Grandma Rose called me Emily."

"When?" asked Natasha.

"The last time we visited. We'd taken her to the common area for bingo, remember? She had that

12

yellow blanket over her lap, because she always got so cold." Ava saw the scene in her mind, Papa standing behind Grandma Rose in her wheelchair while Ava and her sisters perched on folding chairs on either side of her. Ava could practically smell the nursing home's distinct scent, a cloying mix of dying flowers and cleaning products.

Natasha tapped her lower lip. "The prize cart."

"Yes, the prize cart," Ava said. "That's the only reason she wanted to go."

"Grandma Rose does love that prize cart," Darya said.

It was nothing but a metal cart on wheels, the sort librarians used when reshelving books. After each round of bingo, an aide wheeled the cart to the elderly winner, who got to choose from a variety of inexpensive prizes: costume jewelry, bookmarks, little packets of tissues. Sometimes bananas, although what kind of bingo prize was a banana?

"I pretended to sprinkle winning-number fairy dust over her bingo cards," Ava said with a frown. "That's seriously all I did."

"Omigosh, *yes*," Natasha said. "And Grandma Rose sucked in her breath so hard that I thought she was choking."

13

"She said, 'Emily, *no*,' and slapped my hand," Ava said. The slap had stung, but more than that, it had hurt Ava's feelings. It had made her feel like Grandma Rose was a stranger.

"She started, like, rocking in her wheelchair," Natasha said. She moved back and forth, mimicking Grandma Rose. "She picked at her blanket, practically tearing it to pieces—"

"And that bossy aide demanded to know what we'd done to *distress* her," Darya said. Her expression confirmed that she remembered too. "The aide with the huge glasses and big hair, who always smells like onions."

Ava nodded.

"She told us we should leave, because clearly we'd *overexcited* her," Darya continued. "I was like, 'Where do you get off, acting like you know what's better for our grandmother than we do?'"

"We did leave, though," mused Natasha.

"And we haven't been back since," said Darya. She frowned. "That's really sad."

It *was* sad, Ava thought. Maybe, after her Wishing Day, she'd ask Papa to take them to visit her.

"But it was the fairy dust that upset her," Ava said. Goose bumps rose over her arms. "Because, you know . . . magic."

Her sisters didn't respond for several seconds. Then Natasha cleared her throat and said, "Aunt Elena *is* trying to make Mama go see Papa."

"You're changing the subject," Ava said.

"She agrees that it's ridiculous how Mama keeps living in denial," Natasha persevered.

"Only I think we're *all* living in denial," Ava said. She slid her hands under her thighs, determined not to fidget. "But once we find out the truth about Emily, there won't be anything left to deny."

"*Ava . . . ,*" said Natasha.

Ava's breath caught. "No. Don't say my name like that."

"I do want our family to be a family again, Mama included," Natasha said.

"Yes! Good!"

"And maybe you're right about Mama. Maybe, until she finds out what happened to Emily, she won't be able to come back to us for real."

"*Yes!* Which is why—"

"But if, once upon a time, there *was* an Emily, there isn't an Emily now," Natasha concluded. She maintained eye contact for barely a moment before looking away. She rose to her feet and brushed the dirt

15

from her jeans. "I've got to go. I'm meeting Stanley at Rocky's Diner."

A lump formed in Ava's throat. "Meeting your boyfriend is more important than this?"

Natasha studied Ava with an expression Ava couldn't interpret. "Ava, I'm going to ask you a question that you're not going to like."

"Fantastic. That sounds awesome."

Natasha continued to look at her, and Ava felt a jolt of recognition. *Pity.* Natasha was looking at her with pity.

"Omigosh," Ava said. "Just ask."

Natasha squatted so that she was at Ava's eye level. She propped her elbows on her knees and stacked her forearms. One small nudge from Ava, and over Natasha would go.

"You think you're the only one who can solve our family's problems," Natasha stated. "I understand why you feel that way. I *love* you for feeling that way."

Ava waited.

"The thing is," Natasha continued, "are they actually your problems to solve?"

Ava almost laughed. *This* was Natasha's big question? The absurdity of it, combined with Natasha's earnestness, made it tempting to tease her sister. Maybe she'd poke Natasha after all, just to see her topple over.

"Um, yeah, they *are* my problems to solve," she said, trying to keep a *duh* inflection from her tone.

Her reasoning was simple. On the third day of the third month after a girl's thirteenth birthday, every girl in Willow Hill got to make three wishes: an impossible wish, a wish she could make come true herself, and the deepest wish of her most secret heart.

Natasha had made her wishes.

Darya had made her wishes.

Ava was the only sister with wishes left to use, as Natasha well knew. If Ava didn't fix things, who would?

"You don't understand what I'm saying," Natasha said. "What I mean is, did you make Mama abandon us when we were little kids?"

No more laughter.

"Mama didn't *abandon* us," Ava said. Except she had, and Ava knew it. All three sisters knew it.

"Did you make Emily disappear?" Natasha persisted.

Ava stared at her lap.

"And Ava, even if you did cause any of this, which you didn't, what if there *is* no way to make things better?"

"I'm not a baby," Ava said under her breath. She could sense her sisters glancing at each other over her head.

17

"Sorry, what?" Natasha said.

"I'm not cute or adorable or someone who just . . . floats through life."

"You're muttering. I can't understand you."

"Too bad, so sad," Ava said, barely moving her lips.

Natasha placed her hand on Ava's shoulder. Ava's chest rose and fell.

"Ava, it's going to be okay," Natasha said.

"How can you say that when you just said there's no way to fix things?" Ava cried. "My Wishing Day is in *two days*." She gripped her journal and shook it. "That's why I brought this, so we could come up with ideas, and I could write them down. Ideas for what to wish for!"

"Listen to me," Natasha said firmly. "Whatever you wish for will be the right thing."

"You just said it won't be! You said I can't make anything better, so why should I even try?"

Natasha sighed heavily. "Just . . . do what feels right at the time. Trust yourself. I do."

"Natasha!" Ava wailed.

Natasha gave Ava a hug. She even kissed the top of her head. Then she pushed herself up, ducked through the willow's branches, and was gone.

Darya rose next, finger-combing her hair and

announcing that she had plans with her friend Tally.

"Wait, what?" Ava said. "You can't leave, too!"

"Natasha's right," Darya said. "It's not your job to take on all the world's problems."

"It *is* my job to take on our family's problems. Our *whole* family's problems." Ava lowered her voice, even though Natasha was out of hearing range. "You know what I'm talking about."

Darya hovered on one foot, then the other.

"The picture Tally drew," Ava said. "I kept waiting for you to tell Natasha. When you didn't, I figured . . . I don't know. That for whatever reason, you weren't ready to."

"Excellent deduction," Darya said.

"But Tally's your best friend, just like Emily was Mama's best friend!"

"Don't bring Tally into this," Darya warned.

"Tally already *is* in this! And Tally's mother—"

"Has been in and out of mental hospitals Tally's whole life," Darya interrupted. "She's not 'eccentric' like Great-Grandma Elnora. She's got schizophrenia. She can't tell what's real and what's not."

"'She can't tell what's real and what's not,'" Ava repeated. She half laughed. "Do you even hear your-self? Can *any* of us tell what's real and what's not?"

19

Darya glanced past Ava at some indeterminate location.

"Oh, come on," Ava said. "It's got to be the *hugest coincidence in the world* that Tally was placed here, in Willow Hill, with her new foster parents. Unless, that is, it *wasn't* a coincidence."

"Drop it, Ava."

"But *you* found the picture. You figured out who it was a picture *of.*"

"And I decided to leave it alone!" snapped Darya. "You're clinging to the past just as much as Mama, Ava. But guess what? Tally wants to move forward— and so do I."

Darya spun on her heel and pushed through the willow's fronds, leaving Ava alone and bewildered. She wanted to move forward, too. She did. Just, she wanted that for *everybody*, with no one left behind.

Beneath the willow tree, Ava uncapped her pen. She opened her journal and considered the blank page before her. A honeybee buzzed in a meandering path in front of her, and Ava considered it instead.

Hi, little bee, she thought. *What about you? Do you have any brilliant ideas to pass along?*

The bee stopped midflight, rotating to face her and hovering in a single spot, looking for all the world as if it was returning her gaze. Just before Ava was convinced that something truly odd was going on—something magical, even—the bee zipped off.

Ava couldn't help but laugh, and laughing was good. It created room between her ribs.

A moment later, the bee hummed past her again, coming from the opposite direction. *Well, hello again, little bee*, Ava said silently. *Did you forget something?*

She smiled at the thought of the honeybee returning to its hive for a bee-sized cell phone or wallet. Or . . . what? A good luck charm for collecting pollen? A kiss from its honeybee honeybun? Maybe even honeybees made mistakes the first time around.

She caught her breath, a preposterous idea buzzing into her mind. She examined it from multiple angles, then gripped her pen and bent over her notebook, scribbling down her thoughts before she could convince herself not to.

The facts:

*When Mama was thirteen, she made a bad wish.
  She made her best friend disappear.
*Her best friend's name was Emily.
*Emily was also Papa's little sister.

*Mama went mad with guilt, and eventually, she
  decided she couldn't take it anymore. So she left.
*Now she's back, but I think she feels so guilty
  about everything that she's stuck in the past. I
  think she does want to move forward, but can't. I
  don't think she'll be able to until somebody rights
  the long-ago wrong that led to this mess.
*In other words, somebody has to do a do-over—
  and that somebody is me. That someone can <u>only</u>
  be me.

Ava drew her notebook to her chest and hugged it
close. What needed to be done was impossible, but Ava
didn't let herself dwell on that.

Impossible situations called for impossible solutions.

That's what wishes were for.

I wish I could find a way to heal.

—Nathaniel Blok, age thirty-eight

CHAPTER TWO

Ava

"Angela, won't you have some more corn bread?" Aunt Vera asked, and Ava quietly ripped her napkin into shreds beneath the table.

"Absolutely," Angela said, accepting the bread bowl. "It's delicious."

It was delicious, but tonight the corn bread stuck in Ava's throat. Family dinners were supposed to be for *family*. When Ava had returned home that evening, however, she'd seen Angela's cheerful blue pickup truck parked behind Papa's ancient tan pickup truck, which was dented and scratched. He used his truck to transport the lutes he made in his wood shop to the art fairs where he sold them, the same art fairs that

Angela frequented with her handcrafted jewelry.

Ava had spent hours in Papa's truck, sometimes in the cracked vinyl passenger seat in the front, sometimes in the back with the lutes. She wasn't supposed to ride in the bed of the truck. No seat belts and all that. But Papa said kids used to always ride in the backs of pickup trucks, so he let her, if the route was on country roads and not highways. Ava loved the freedom of riding in the open air, her hair whipping around and the warm sun bringing out the tingly scent of the linseed oil Papa buffed the lutes with.

Ava loved Papa's dented-up old truck. She did. But Angela's blue truck was SO CUTE. Ava felt disloyal for thinking such a thing, but there was no denying it. Equally undeniable? How cool it was that Angela, all delicate bangles and dangly earrings, drove a truck, period.

Ava wouldn't mind driving such a truck one day.

Ava would adore driving such a truck one day.

And if Mama were here, and Angela were for sure just a friend of the family, Ava would gush over Angela's truck and maybe ask if Angela would give her a ride in it.

But Mama wasn't here. Neither was Aunt Elena, who, if she were present, could run interference and do all she could to remind Papa that he was already taken.

Not just "taken." He was married!

Instead, Angela was here, and she'd clearly taken care with her makeup and her outfit. She wore perfume that smelled like what Ava imagined the ocean smelled like, fresh and exhilarating. Ava wanted to hate it, but couldn't.

And Aunt Vera! Aunt Vera was Mama's older sister, and yet all evening long, Aunt Vera had treated Angela like a welcome guest. She seemed *pleased* that Papa was coming out of his long hibernation. If only Aunt Vera knew that Mama was back in Willow Hill! Rather than offering Angela more corn bread, maybe she'd throw a piece at her.

Well, no, Aunt Vera would never throw corn bread at anyone. But maybe she wouldn't fawn over Angela, refilling her iced tea and making polite conversation.

Ava stabbed a spear of asparagus with the tines of her fork, accidentally scraping the china plate.

"Ow!" Darya cried, pressing her hands to her ears.

"I'm sorry, I'm sorry!" said Ava. She tried to be mindful of the fork-on-plate thing. Everyone did, for Darya's sake. "I'll be more careful!"

"It's okay," Darya said, still wincing. "Just, it really does hurt. It's like an ice pick in my head."

Angela looked concerned and interested, both. "Do other sounds hurt your ears, too? Fingernails on a chalkboard, that sort of thing?"

"We don't have chalkboards anymore," Darya said. "We have Smart Boards. But yeah, pretty much any sound that's high-pitched. Also, Jolly Rancher wrappers. When people unwrap Jolly Ranchers, I think I'm going to throw up."

"Jolly Rancher wrappers?" Ava said. This was news to her. She felt weird knowing that she and Angela were both learning this for the first time. She felt . . . like a bad sister, somehow.

"And those dried wasabi peas," Darya went on. "When people bring them for lunch, and they make that squeaky, crunchy sound?" She shuddered. "I have to get up and leave."

"Maybe you have misophonia!" Angela exclaimed, sounding delighted.

"Misophonia?" Darya said.

"Do you hear sounds that other people don't?"

"Sometimes I'll hear a refrigerator humming when no one else can," Darya said dubiously. "That sound doesn't hurt, though."

Angela nodded as if every word out of Darya's mouth was a gem. "Highly sensitive people are more sensitive to the world around them," she said. "Highly sensitive people are also likely to have vivid dreams and be quite artistic."

28

"I guess my dreams are vivid," Darya said. "I'm not artistic, though. My friend Tally? *She's* artistic. She's an *amazing* artist."

Ava's eyes flew to Darya. Darya's cheeks reddened.

"Well, your father tells me you're very creative," Angela said. She smiled at Papa and touched his arm.

Ava shoved back her chair. "May I please be excused?" she asked. She didn't wait for a response, just picked up her plate and utensils and headed out of the dining room and into the kitchen. "Thanks for the—" She broke off. *Thanks for the delicious dinner,* that's what the girls usually said to Aunt Vera.

"Thanks for dinner," Ava said. She was being petty, and she was ashamed of herself. After all, it wasn't as if Angela had claimed the word "delicious" for her sole usage. She couldn't, even if she wanted to. "It was really good."

As Ava rinsed her dishes, she heard a soft knock on the back door. Ava slid her plate into the dishwasher and curiously flipped on the outside light.

She froze. Then she shook herself and flung open the door. "Mama!"

Mama smiled nervously, placing her finger over her lips.

"Sorry, right," Ava said, dropping her voice. "But . . . hi! Come in!"

Mama slipped in, more of a scuttle than a step. She wore faded jeans, a soft white T-shirt, and red shoes styled like ballet slippers. She had on red lipstick, too. A slender gold necklace circled her neck, a single rose-colored pearl resting in the hollow of her throat.

"You look so pretty," Ava whispered. Her heart thumped like crazy. Gesturing at the platter in Mama's hands, she said, "And you made brownies! Papa's favorite!"

"How do you remember my brownies, silly girl?" Mama asked with a smile.

"Because Papa talks about them! Well, he hasn't in a while, but—"

From the dining room, Angela's happy laugh rang out. "Nate!" she said playfully. "That's very sweet. Girls, do you know what a sweet man your father is?"

The color drained from Mama's face. Her eyes looked wide and afraid.

"Mama, please don't leave," Ava pleaded, reaching instinctively for her.

Mama backed away, shaking her head. She pushed open the screen door with her hip and stepped outside.

"Mama, *please.*"

"Who is she?" Mama asked.

"No one!"

"She isn't no one. What's her name?"

"Angela, but she's just a friend. She and Papa go to art fairs together."

"They . . . go to art fairs together," Mama repeated.

"Not like on dates or anything. They're just always at the same fairs at the same time!"

"I see," Mama said faintly.

"Ava?" Papa called from the kitchen.

"One sec!" Ava called. Should she pull Mama into the house? Should she physically grab her and hold on to her?

Mama thrust the brownies at her, and then she was gone, the screen door thumping behind her.

Ava heard Papa's heavy footsteps. She pivoted away from the back door.

"Ava," Papa said. "I came to check on you, because you seemed . . ." He rubbed the back of his neck. "Are you upset about something, honey?"

Ava shook her head.

He put his hand on her shoulder. "I know—well, or maybe I *don't*. I don't want to put words in your mouth." The weight of his love made her want to cry. "But it can be confusing to be a teenager. And with your mother gone . . ."

She's not gone! Ava wanted to say. *She was just here!*

"Do you like Angela, sweetheart?" Papa asked, and his vulnerability broke Ava's heart. He *was* moving on. He *was* finding happiness again. What was Ava supposed to do? Stomp her feet and throw a fit? Tell him she *didn't* like Angela, even though she probably secretly did, or could, if it weren't for everything else going on?

"Here," Ava said, handing him the plate of brownies. Her voice hitched. "For dessert."

Papa's face lit up. "Brownies!" He raised his voice. "Ava made brownies, everyone!"

"Oh, *won*derful!" Angela caroled.

"You're a good kid, Ava," Papa said, shifting the brownies to one hand and giving Ava a one-armed hug.

"You're a good papa, Papa," Ava whispered, wrapping her arms around his waist and pressing her face to his shirt. He gave her one more squeeze before heading back to the dining room.

"You coming?" he said, glancing over his shoulder.

She forced herself to smile. "Be right there."

CHAPTER THREE

Ava

That night, after Angela left, Ava got to the den first and claimed the TV. She used the remote to scroll through menus and punch in selections, and within minutes, the movie she'd picked was playing.

"*Back to the Future?*" Stanley said half an hour later, following Natasha into the room. He must have come over after dinner. He dropped onto the other end of the sofa, and after a moment, Natasha sat down between them.

"I watched this three times in a row the first time I saw it," Stanley said. "Can we join you?"

"You already have," Ava pointed out.

"Oh," said Stanley. "True. Do you want us to leave?"

"It's fine," she said. Ava liked Stanley. He was tall and lanky and shy, though he'd grown less so over time. Most importantly, he treated Natasha well.

"Awesome," he said, and right away started reciting lines along with the characters. When Doc Brown showed up in his DeLorean, he laughed and said, *"Yes."*

Ava wondered if DeLoreans existed in real life—sleek, sporty cars with doors that opened up instead of out. She'd never seen one. She'd remember if she had.

"Gull wings," Stanley said.

"Huh?" said Ava.

"The doors. They're called that because they resemble the wings of a gull."

"Huh," said Ava.

"It makes the car more streamlined. Better for time travel."

"Ah. Well, of course," Ava said. She and Natasha shared an amused glance. Still, Ava made a mental note: *Streamlined. Okay.*

"Do you know why else Doc built his time machine using a DeLorean?" Stanley asked.

"Please tell us," Natasha teased.

"For a couple of reasons. First, the DeLorean is

constructed from stainless steel. That was crucial in terms of creating the flux capacitor."

Ava perked up. She knew that the flux capacitor was the Important Thing that allowed Doc Brown and Marty McFly to go back in time, but that was all she knew. Stanley kept talking, using terms like "rear-mounted two-point-eight-five-liter blah-blah-PRV engine," "fiberglass body structure," and, bewilderingly, "a steel backbone."

"Do you know why Doc was so particular about every detail?" Stanley asked.

"Because he wanted to get it right?" Ava guessed.

"To increase his chances of having a smooth passage through the space-time continuum," said Stanley.

Ava sat up straighter. After her epiphany beneath the willow tree, she'd stopped by the public library and pored over scientific articles exploring the possibility of time travel. Gravitational field equations, something called Tensor Calculus, Einstein's theory of general relativity . . .

The reading had been dense and had made her brain hurt. She'd decided to watch *Back to the Future* in the hopes of finding an easier way to unravel the mysteries of time travel. She knew it was just a movie, but still.

On the television screen, Marty McFly was having a soda with George McFly, who would one day be Marty's father—unless Marty screwed things up.

"Do physicists really believe in that thing you just said?" Ava concentrated on getting the term right. "Space-time continuums?"

Stanley grinned. "Sure they do. So do I, and I'm not even a physicist."

"And the concept of a space-time continuum means thinking of the world not as three-dimensional, but as four-dimensional," Ava said, furrowing her brow. "Is that right?"

Natasha gave her a funny look.

"That's a simplified way of describing it, but yeah," Stanley said. "We exist in space. Space is three-dimensional, with height, width, and depth."

"Unlike a painting, which is two-dimensional," Ava said.

"Actually, a painting is still three-dimensional. You can hold a painting, right? Like if you were hanging it on the wall?"

"Well, yeah."

"But the image *represented* in the painting is two-dimensional. If it's a painting of a bridge, for example—"

"The bridge in the painting is two-dimensional," Ava said. "Got it. And since I'm three-dimensional, I couldn't walk over the bridge, even if it were life-size."

"Guys? The movie?" said Natasha.

Ava scooted forward on the sofa, leaning past Natasha to better see Stanley. "But *time* is different. It's not height or width or depth. That's why it's called the fourth dimension?"

"It's more complicated than that, but that's a decent starting point," Stanley said. "You, Ava, are three-dimensional, like you said. Same for me, same for Natasha, same for the sofa. But for us to exist, we have to exist some*where*, although 'where' isn't the right word. It's more that we have to exist some*when*."

Somewhen. Ava's skin tingled.

"Without time, there couldn't be space. There couldn't be *us*." Stanley held Ava's gaze. "Time is the fabric that makes space possible."

Ava silently repeated his words, memorizing them.

"Ava, you look like you're studying for an exam," Natasha said with a laugh.

"What about wormholes?" Ava asked. "Physicists say that a person could travel through a wormhole to go forward or backward in time. Is that right?"

"Okay, whoa," said Natasha.

"In theory," Stanley answered. "The problem is that wormholes collapse once matter enters them."

"What's a *wormhole*?" Natasha asked. "And Ava? Why are you suddenly interested in this stuff?"

Prickles at the back of Ava's neck cautioned her to be careful. At the same time, talking about all this was exciting. Unlike Natasha and Darya, Stanley was giving her real answers to her real questions. He was taking her seriously.

To Natasha, she said, "Pretend you have Aunt Vera's tape measure, the soft one she uses for sewing, and you're holding it tight." She demonstrated, pinching an invisible tape measure between her thumbs and index fingers and stretching it taut. "If you wanted to go from point A"—she indicated the left end of the pretend tape measure—"to point B"—she wiggled her right hand—"you'd walk across it. Easy-peasy."

"If you were an ant," said Natasha.

"If the tape measure was twelve inches long, you'd have to walk the entire twelve inches. But there's a faster way." Ava brought her hands together so that the invisible tape measure hung in a loop. "Now you, or the ant, can go from point A to point B in one step. See?"

"Not bad," Stanley said. "Ava just might turn out

to be a scientist, Natasha."

"But wormholes *collapse*," Natasha said. "You said so, Stanley."

"They do, like how caves sometimes collapse on coal miners," Stanley said. "That's the problem: figuring out how to make wormholes stable enough to travel through."

"And?" demanded Natasha.

Stanley shrugged. "It's impossible. Well, so far."

Natasha looked pointedly at Ava, who turned her attention to the TV, where Marty McFly winced as a bully humiliated his future dad.

"So time travel is *impossible*," Natasha clarified. "Right, Stanley?"

"You would die," Stanley replied. "Yes."

"Do you hear that, Ava?" Natasha said. She raised her voice. "*Ava.*"

Ava startled, pretending she'd gotten so absorbed in the movie that she'd lost track of the conversation. Then she adopted a solicitous expression, as if humoring an elderly relative. "Right," she said. "Time travel is impossible. Traveling through a wormhole would kill me."

"Good," Natasha said.

Ava sank back into the sofa. Flux capacitors,

wormholes, the space-time continuum—it was helpful information, even though Ava was sure any traveling she did wouldn't involve a DeLorean.

As for the "it's impossible" bit? She silently recited her new mantra: *Impossible situations require impossible solutions.*

I wish people would quit thinking that saying
"It's complicated" makes things any better.
—AVA BLOK, AGE THIRTEEN, THREE MONTHS, AND
TWO DAYS

CHAPTER FOUR

Ava

The next morning, Natasha and Darya cornered Ava in her room.

"Tomorrow is your Wishing Day," Natasha informed her.

"It *is?*" Ava exclaimed. "Wow. How time flies!"

"Ha, ha," Darya said. "Speaking of, that's why we're here. You are expressly forbidden from trying anything stupid like that yourself."

"Like what?" Ava asked innocently. She allowed the *you're forbidden* part to slide. Although what in the world made Natasha and Darya think they could *forbid* her from anything?

"Like flying through time, dum-dum," Darya said, flicking Ava's head.

"Like wishing to go to the past," Natasha said. "I told Darya about your sudden fascination with science, and *no*."

"I can't be fascinated by science?"

Darya put her hands on her hips. "You can be fascinated with science all you want. What you *can't* do is wish for a blowhole or whatever to open up and suck you through time."

"Oh, please, I would never," Ava said. A blowhole, after all, was the hole whales used to blow air out of water. Although . . . *hmm*. The image of ocean spray spouting from a whale made bubbles fizz and pop in her brain. Water. Air. Diving deep into water and leaping into the air. And babies, *human* babies, breathed water before they were born, didn't they? Then, when it was time, out they popped into the air, born into a new and different world?

"We're not trying to be bossy," Natasha said.

You're not? Ava thought.

"Just, we love you, and we want you to stay safe."

"I love you, too," Ava said, and she meant it. Her intentions were as love-based as theirs. "Of course I'll be safe."

44

"Also, I've said it already, but I'm going to say it again," Darya said. "Leave Tally out of it."

Like you did last night at dinner? Ava was tempted to say. *How you went on and on about Tally's amazing artistic ability, the ability that made it possible for Tally to draw such striking likenesses of real, live people?*

Instead, she saluted Darya and said, "Heard and understood, Sergeant." Darya could interpret her remark however she chose.

It was a Saturday, which meant no school. After scarfing down a toasted bagel slathered with cream cheese, she snuck Aunt Vera's iPad into her backpack and escaped to do more research. Tomorrow was indeed her Wishing Day, as her sisters had so helpfully pointed out.

At Rocky's, an old-fashioned diner with swivel chairs and booths with red benches, Ava ordered a chocolate milkshake and took it to a high, round table, where she hiked herself onto a tall stool. She took a long sip of her shake and pulled out her aunt's iPad. She considered, for a moment, the unexpectedness of stodgy Aunt Vera even *owning* an iPad.

Aunt Elena, Mama and Aunt Vera's youngest sister, had given the iPad to Aunt Vera on Aunt Vera's most recent birthday. Aunt Vera had pooh-poohed it until Natasha walked her through the basics and showed her how to connect to the internet. Now Aunt Vera adored it.

She wouldn't miss it for a few hours, though. Aunt Vera went to the farmers' market every Saturday. She spent eons there.

A quick glance at Aunt Vera's browser history told Ava that Aunt Vera was mainly interested in recipes. That came as no surprise. With Mama gone, Aunt Vera continued to do most of the cooking for Nate and the girls.

Ava discovered that Aunt Vera also appeared to be addicted to an old TV show called *Charmed*. That *was* a surprise. Aunt Vera hardly ever watched TV, unless it was a PBS special or a live broadcast of the Boston Philharmonic Orchestra. Some quick googling revealed that *Charmed* was about three sisters, a missing mother, and *magic*. Magic?!

Never, ever would Ava have guessed that Aunt Vera might watch a show—choose to watch a show—about magic. And not only that, but on the sly! After recovering from the shock, Ava felt a wave of fondness for Aunt Vera. It was cool how people always had more layers than it first appeared. Did Natasha and Darya know that, or would Ava always be their dreamy baby sister?

More googling revealed that the sisters in *Charmed* were witches—"good" witches—who had an ancient spell book called *The Book of Shadows*, which taught them how to fight off demons, warlocks, and other baddies. They also had witchy, paranormal powers, which added another layer of intrigue to Aunt Vera's fondness for the show.

Might Grandma Rose, who seemed as practical as Aunt Vera, harbor a secret fascination for such "non-sense" as well? What if people sometimes claimed to detest the very things they were obsessed with, for fear of how others might perceive them? *Or,* what if people claimed to detest the things they feared, for superstitious reasons of their own?

Ava learned that the youngest sister on *Charmed*, Phoebe, could see both the past and the future. "Premonition" was the name for Phoebe's type of magic. Ava also learned that all three sisters could communicate through telepathy, which meant they could read one another's thoughts.

Ava did a Google search on telepathy. Some people said it was real; others insisted it was a sham. Ava dug deeper. She found a wealth of scholarly articles on telepathy, articles as dense as the ones about time travel that she'd struggled with yesterday at the public library.

Contrary to Ava's expectations, plenty of research supported the claim that rare individuals *could* read the thoughts of others. For example, a neuroscientist with an unpronounceable name set up an experiment in which people in India used electroencephalographs to send thoughts to people in France—and it worked! *Electroencephalographs* was the long name for EEGs. EEGs, Ava learned, were skullcaps made from dozens of small electrodes.

The neuroscientist hooked up matching EEGs to pairs of subjects: one skullcap was placed on a person who lived in India, and the other was placed on someone in France. The subject in India was asked to visualize something specific, like an apple, and the subject in France was asked to draw what he or she saw.

The article spewed out elaborate graphs, statistics, and more long, unpronounceable words. Ava didn't understand much of it, but the takeaway was clear.

"With a relative standard deviation of 2.96, our study provides compelling evidence that no less than one percent of humans demonstrates an accurate and replicable ability to read the thoughts of others," the article concluded. "This phenomenon, termed 'telepathy' in common parlance, is indeed real."

One percent of humans had telepathy, Ava marveled. Scientists said so!

An article in *Yale Scientific* also stated that telepathy couldn't be discounted, and a paper in a journal called *Behavior and Brain Science* suggested that even claims of communication between humans and ghosts shouldn't be rejected out of hand. *Ghosts!* It was mind-blowing!

"Assume, in the name of philosophical consideration, that a 'ghost' is the non-material energy of a person deceased," the author of the paper argued. "If the thoughts of a living human exist without material form, why, then, shouldn't the thoughts of a ghost exist in the same way? The extension of this claim is self-evident: If humans can communicate telepathically when alive, then it is reasonable to assume that humans can communicate telepathically with beings no longer extant."

Ava looked up *extant*. It meant "still alive." So, okay. The author of the paper was using fancy words to say *that humans could communicate with ghosts.*

Wow.

Ava hopped from link to link, falling deeper into

the rabbit hole that was the internet.

She learned that in the olden days, people accused of having telepathy were burned at the stake. She learned that even now, some people considered telepathy to be the devil's work. She read about kids with telepathy who were cast out of their families because the kids' abilities freaked out their parents. She read about adults with telepathy who were diagnosed with mental illness and put on so many medications that they no longer knew their own thoughts, much less the thoughts of others.

Much of what Ava discovered gave her a shuddery feeling at the base of her spine. It also gave her a new perspective about the "magic" said to exist in Willow Hill. Plenty of Willow Hill's residents dismissed the possibility of magic completely: Grandma Rose and Aunt Vera, for example. Others held a friendly "why not?" sort of attitude. Others, like Mama, were true believers.

If Mama's account of what happened after her Wishing Day was true—that Emily was there one day and gone the next—then Ava couldn't blame her.

Ava thought again about Grandma Rose, and from Grandma Rose to Grandpa Dave, who was Papa's father and Grandma Rose's ex-husband. Did Grandpa

Dave remember a once-upon-a-time daughter named Emily? Or, if he didn't, did he slip every so often, the way Grandma Rose did when she'd called Ava "Emily" during their last visit to the nursing home?

Ava blinked, recalling an incident that she must have buried in her subconscious. As the memory rose to the surface, Ava experienced the same burning whiteness she'd felt beneath the willow tree, when she discovered her sisters had kept secrets from her on purpose.

She, Ava, was guilty of the same thing. She'd kept a secret from herself. A big one.

Last September, a couple of months before Darya's Wishing Day, Ava had gone with Papa to an art fair. Darya had gotten up early to help load Papa's lutes into his truck. Nothing strange so far, just a normal morning. But before Papa and Ava set off, Darya asked Ava to bring her back a caramel apple. Again, no big deal. Just one sister asking the other for a favor. But, because Darya was Darya, and Darya was picky, her request for a caramel apple had grown comically specific.

First, she'd said she wanted chocolate and peanuts on top, but not walnuts. Then she clarified that if there weren't any with peanuts, to get one with just caramel and chocolate.

"But not white chocolate, because white chocolate is a scam," Darya had said.

"I'll try," Ava replied, and Darya had said something like, "Um, no, you *will*. If you don't, Papa will leave you behind. Right, Papa?"

Papa, hearing his name, had blinked and said, "What's that?"

Then came the bad part. The not-normal part. Darya said, "Ava has to bring me a caramel apple or you'll disown her. Right?"

Papa had frowned. "Disown her? Why would I disown her?"

"You wouldn't," Darya said. "I was teasing."

"I don't understand," Papa said, and *whoosh*, the mood changed.

"Papa, it was a joke," Darya had said.

"How is it a joke, when I've lost so much already?" Papa had said. He'd turned to Ava with glassy eyes, his expression blank. "I would *never* disown you, Emily. Never."

Ava had lost her words.

Darya had stammered, "Papa, I know. I was just . . . I didn't mean . . ."

Papa had remained not-Papa for several stomach-lurching moments. And at Rocky's Diner, eons after that dreadful moment, Ava felt as if she were on a Tilt-A-Whirl. She remembered how the world had listed sideways as Papa stared at her. Finally, he came back to himself. When he came back, the world came back.

In his normal voice, with a normal expression, he'd asked what the holdup was. Ava had scurried into the truck, heart thumping. Papa cranked the key, and the engine rumbled to life, its familiar thrum steadying Ava's pulse.

Ava had glanced back at Darya as they drove off. Tiny pinpricks of light had blurred her vision, making Darya look hazy and far away.

Ava shut down Aunt Vera's iPad, suddenly weary. If Ava knew without a trace of doubt that Emily existed, or that she'd existed once upon a time, she felt sure she'd find the strength to persevere. If only the universe would send her a sign! Couldn't the universe just . . . send her a sign?!

A waitress jostled the table, tipping over the sugar dispenser.

"Oops, sorry, hon!" the waitress said. "I'll pop right back with a rag."

"No problem," Ava said. Her voice sounded croaky. She cleared her throat and gave the waitress a smile. "I've got it."

Ava righted the container and swept the spilled sugar into her hand. Some of the crystals remained, lodged into strokes gouged into the table.

Ava froze. She squeezed her eyes shut, opened them, and reread the message carved on the old, scarred table. The words were faint, aged by time and grease, but Ava had no trouble making them out: *Klara & Emily, best friends forever.*

Klara was Ava's mother's name.

I wish I knew all the answers.

—THE BIRD LADY

CHAPTER FIVE

Emily, age eight

It wasn't until Emily was eight years old that she knew for sure she wasn't like regular kids. She wondered if she might not be like regular grown-ups, either, except maybe Grandma Elnora. Only, that wasn't a good thing. Emily knew this because of the lines that formed on her mother's face when Emily said something that reminded her mom of Grandma Elnora. When that happened—and Emily had yet to figure out the rules for making it *not* happen—her mother would grab Emily's chin and make Emily look at her.

"No ma'am," her mother would say. "That is *not* how we behave."

Those were the words her mother said in her "out loud" voice. The words she said in her "not out loud" voice were *Please, no. Emily has an active imagination, that's all. Please don't let my baby have my mother's curse!*

A curse was a sickness, and Grandma Elnora, who visited on the first Sunday of every month, had that sickness. It wasn't a tummy ache or the flu. It was . . . well, Emily didn't know *what* it was, except that Grandma Elnora, like Emily, said things she wasn't supposed to.

Like what happened a few weeks ago. Emily, Emily's mom, and Grandma Elnora had gone for a walk. Emily's brother, Nate, stayed home with their dad. Grandma Elnora glanced at Emily as they were heading out the door and said, "You're going to trip if you wear those shoes, sweetness. You'll trip and ruin your pretty dress."

"Mother, please," Emily's mom said. To Emily, she said, "Your shoes are perfect. They make you look like a little lady."

Emily looked down at her shiny black shoes. They were called Mary Janes, and they had a strap and a buckle. They pinched Emily's toes.

During their walk, Emily *did* trip. She went

58

sprawling onto the sidewalk, and she *did* ruin her pretty dress. She ripped the hem and got dirt on it, too.

"*Mother!*" snapped Emily's mom. She was so mad she forgot to hug Emily and check on her bleeding knee.

"What?" Grandma Elnora said. "*I* didn't make her trip, Rose. Emily, darling, did I make you trip?"

Emily shook her head, hot tears building up behind her eyes. She'd tripped all on her own. She had a scab for a week. She pulled it off before the skin underneath was ready, and she touched the moistness of it with the tip of her finger. Then she touched her finger to her tongue. Salty.

And another time:

Just last Sunday, Emily's mother baked brownies when Grandma Elnora came over. While they were in the oven, Grandma Elnora said, "Rose, you need to take them out, or they're going to burn."

"Mother, I am quite capable of making brownies without your input," Emily's mom retorted from the sofa. That's what she said with her out loud words. Inside her head, her mother wondered if she should check on them, just to be sure.

She didn't.

I know full well how to set a timer, Emily heard her say silently. *I am an* excellent *baker*. Her mother's unspoken words were accompanied by a wave of emotion, which Emily also sensed. Emily's mom didn't want Grandma Elnora to "win." She didn't want Grandma Elnora to be right.

Emily's mom checked her watch. She tapped her foot. She rose the moment the timer beeped, but it was too late. The unmistakable smell of burnt brownies wafted into the den, and Emily's mom cried out and stamped her foot.

Grandma Elnora caught Emily's gaze and lifted her eyebrows. *I tell her and tell her,* she said to Emily with silent words. *Is it my fault if she doesn't listen?*

At school, Emily gathered more clues that told her she was different from others. In third grade, she heard a girl named Sophie silently wishing she had hair like Klara Kosrov's. Klara was another girl in their class. Emily looked at Klara's hair, which was long and straight and shiny. She looked at Sophie's hair, which was blondish and cut very short.

"Klara's hair *is* pretty," Emily told Sophie. "But yours is, too."

Sophie's eyes widened. She felt embarrassed and ashamed—those were the emotions that washed over Emily—and she scurried away even as Emily cried, "No, wait! Come back!"

Something similar happened with her third-grade teacher, Mrs. Robinson. In February, Mrs. Robinson had started growing distracted during lesson time, losing her train of thought and standing at the chalkboard looking dazed. While Mrs. Robinson was grading papers, she worried about her father, who was in the hospital. Sometimes she pictured him in his hospital bed, which made Mrs. Robinson sad. Other times she imagined him in his garden, which made her sad in a different way. When Mrs. Robinson thought of her father in his garden, Emily saw what she saw: a stooped man with big ears and a kind face, scattering mulch around a bed of flowers.

Please let him get better, Mrs. Robinson thought. *Please let this new medication work.*

Emily made a get-well card for Mrs. Robinson's father, drawing a bouquet of flowers exactly like the flowers in Mrs. Robinson's father's garden. Emily was good at art.

"For your father," she explained when Mrs. Robinson drew in a sharp breath. She tried to hold on to her smile, but Mrs. Robinson's expression made Emily scurry away, just as Emily, without meaning to, had made Sophie scurry away by complimenting Sophie's hair.

From that point on, Mrs. Robinson treated Emily the way she might treat an unfamiliar dog, a creature that might or might not bite. Emily felt confused and . . . and *scolded*, although Mrs. Robinson didn't scold Emily out loud.

One day, not long after Emily had given Mrs. Robinson the card, the third graders had recess in the gymnasium because it was raining outside. Pouring, really, the sky a dark, bruised color.

Emily spotted Mrs. Robinson talking to the other third-grade teacher by a stack of foam mats, and warning bells pealed in Emily's head.

She strolled in a wide loop around the gym, making certain her path took her by the two teachers. She tried to be invisible, *la la la, just walking around the gym*. When Emily passed Mrs. Robinson and Mrs. Singh, they stopped talking. She continued several feet farther, then knelt and pretended to tie her shoe. The teachers returned to their conversation, their voices low.

"She told me the card was for my father," Mrs. Robinson murmured. "It was sweet, I suppose. But how did she know my father was sick?"

"Did you mention it to the students?" Mrs. Singh asked.

"I didn't."

"Perhaps something slipped out," Mrs. Singh suggested. "It happens, you know."

"Maybe you're right," Mrs. Robinson fretted. "Of course you're right. And I *like* Emily. She's bright, creative, polite . . ." She fingered the cross she wore around her neck. "But tell me this, Louise. Have you ever sensed something *unnatural* about her?"

Face burning, Emily straightened up and strode away.

She'd learned something, however. She'd been given an important piece of the puzzle. *Mrs. Robinson didn't understand how Emily knew about her father's illness, because Mrs. Robinson hadn't mentioned it out loud.*

Emily thought back to the day with Sophie. Emily had complimented Sophie's hair to make Sophie feel better, because Sophie had wished she had hair like Klara Kosrov's instead. Only, like Mrs. Robinson, Sophie hadn't said what she'd been thinking *out loud*.

Was it as simple as that? Were you only supposed to talk to people when the conversation was out loud?

She tested her theory, holding back from responding when people *thought* something but didn't *say* it. One day Emily noticed a frail girl named Lucy crouched over her saddle oxfords, coloring in the black bits with black Magic Marker. Emily felt Lucy's anxiety, and she saw what Lucy saw: other kids laughing and pointing, making fun of her for being too poor to buy new shoes. Emily wanted to tell Lucy that no one was thinking about her shoes at all, but she kept her mouth shut.

Likewise, Emily almost exclaimed over how awesome it was that Maggie Stanton's parents gave Maggie a kitten for her birthday. A super-cute kitten, which Emily knew because Maggie couldn't stop thinking about her. Black with white paws, like little white mittens. Emily smiled, wanting to tell Maggie that yes, Mittens was a great name for her kitten.

She stopped herself in time, just barely.

Emily messed up with a boy named John Blasingame, though. John had always been grumpy, standoffish, the kind of boy whose body language told other kids to stay away. One morning, Emily found out why. She stood behind him, waiting to use the pencil sharpener, and his gray thoughts scuttled over her.

John was scared of his dad. He kept seeing his dad's hard eyes and drawn-back fist. Emily, seeing what he saw, felt a pang.

"If your dad's hurting you, you should tell Mrs. Robinson," she blurted.

John went pale. Fear flickered in his eyes. Then his skin grew red and mottled, and Emily's stomach dropped.

"Leave me alone, weirdo," he said.

From then on, she stayed as far away from John as she could.

All of those incidents, considered together, made her think her theory was right, though. She didn't understand why—or why no one had bothered to teach her—but the rule seemed to be that she should speak only when spoken to. In other words, she shouldn't speak when *thoughtened* to. *Thoughten* probably wasn't a real word, but whatever.

Still, there had to be more to it than that. Emily's mom, for example, didn't like it when Emily knew things the way Grandma Elnora knew things, even if whatever it was didn't come up in conversation.

Maybe it was impolite for a person to let on in any way, shape, or form that she or he knew what another person was thinking? Although again, if that were the case, why hadn't her mom simply told her so, the way she told Emily to chew with her mouth closed and keep her dinner napkin in her lap?

An alarming idea occurred to Emily. What if certain people, like her mom and Mrs. Robinson and

John Blasingame, didn't have to "pretend" not to know what other people were thinking? What if certain people honestly *couldn't* hear other people's thoughts?

Was it possible?

Some people were good at basketball. Other people—like Emily—couldn't make a basket to save their lives. From what Emily was stitching together, maybe the same was true when it came to reading people's thoughts. Maybe Emily and Grandma Elnora had a talent for it, just by luck of the draw. Grandma Elnora also had the talent of seeing the future, like with the brownies and Emily's ripped dress. Emily *didn't* have that talent.

More bits and bobs came together. The dread in Emily's stomach grew.

Because parents *liked* it when their kids won basketball games or got first prize in a spelling bee. Parents admired those sorts of talents. So did other grown-ups. So did kids.

Nobody admired Emily's talent.

As a matter of fact, other than Grandma Elnora, no one understood Emily's talent, or even seemed to think it *was* a talent. "Unnatural" was the word Mrs. Robinson had used. "Leave me alone, weirdo!" John Blasingame had spat.

"Dave, it is our responsibility to teach Emily *to be*

normal," she overheard her mom say to her dad one evening. "We have to encourage her to blend in. What about that don't you understand?"

"Encourage her or force her?" her dad responded. "Emily is Emily. It is *not* our responsibility, or even our prerogative, to turn her into someone else."

Emily didn't know what "prerogative" meant, but a quick probe into her dad's thoughts cleared it up. He was saying that he and her mom didn't have the right to change her into someone she wasn't. More than that, he was saying that he loved Emily just the way she was.

Her eyes stung. She loved him, too. So much.

"Don't play dumb," her mom told her dad. "Maybe Emily doesn't realize how different she is, but other people certainly do—and one day she's bound to find out. The world is cruel, Dave. Do you want our daughter to be a social pariah?"

Pariah, another new word. From her mother, Emily gleaned that it meant an outcast, a person everybody hated.

Hated?

Her lungs constricted, but she stayed very still in the hallway, taking shallow breaths and digging her fingernails into her palms. If her parents knew she was listening, they'd stop talking about her. They might stop thinking about her, too. Or try to.

"I want our daughter to be proud of who she is," her father replied. "Emily won't be a pariah unless you make her see herself as one."

"So this is *my* fault?" her mother said. "It's wrong to want other people to look at us and see a normal, happy family?"

"Rose," her dad said heavily. "Is there such a thing as a 'normal, happy family'?"

"You know what I mean."

"Our family is perfect just as we are," her dad said. "Or we would be, if you'd lay off trying to change everybody."

Emily slunk off, her face burning. Her mom wasn't trying to change *everybody*. Just her.

She waited for her parents to go to bed, then slipped out of her room and went to her brother. Nate was ten and in the fifth grade. He was the best big brother ever. And, like her dad, Nate never treated her like she was weird.

"Hey, Nate, will you play a game with me?" she asked.

He propped himself up on his elbow and put aside his book. "It's late," he said. "We're supposed to be asleep."

"It won't take long. Anyway, you weren't sleeping. You were reading."

He gave her a sideways smile. "Fine. What's the game?"

She perched on the end of his twin-size bed. He scooted back and sat all the way up.

"I'm going to think about something really hard, and I want you to guess what it is," she instructed. "Okay?"

She scrunched her forehead and thought about doughnuts. Doughnuts, doughnuts, doughnuts, because Nate loved doughnuts. She painted the most vivid mental picture she could of his favorite kind: a cake doughnut with maple frosting.

"Well?" she asked. "What was I thinking?"

"That . . . you need to use the bathroom?"

"No!" She wanted to throw something at him, but found nothing to throw. "I was thinking about *doughnuts*. Maple doughnuts." She pushed her hand through her hair. "You think about something, and I'll see if I can tell."

Emily had developed a habit of tuning Nate's thoughts out. She could do that if she tried. She followed the same practice with her mom and dad, although she made exceptions, obviously. It was pretty easy with Nate and her dad. Her mom's thoughts, however, were often so strong that she couldn't keep them out even when she wanted to.

Now, sitting on Nate's bed, she opened herself to his thoughts on purpose.

"You're thinking about the library," she said. "About that desk with walls you sit in, wearing those huge headphones."

"It's called a carrel," Nate said. "I borrow the headphones and a tape player—"

"And listen to that music you like," Emily finished. "Music played on an old-fashioned instrument. Not a guitar, not a mandolin . . ."

Nate started to answer, but Emily cut him off.

"Don't tell me! Just think the word really hard." She closed her eyes, then opened them and grinned. "*Lute!* You listen to lute music!"

Nate tugged at the neck of his pajama shirt, but didn't contradict her.

"Do another," Emily said.

After a moment, she exclaimed, "The field trip you went on to hear a string quartet!"

Nate nodded. He pulled his eyebrows together, and Emily concentrated.

"Mom and Dad," she said. "You're thinking about how . . ." She trailed off. He was thinking about how they'd been fighting more and more. He was also telling Emily that it wasn't her fault. That he'd known for a long time that she was different. That he, like their dad, didn't care.

"But why?" she said. "*Why* am I different?"

"You can read people's minds," he stated.

"You can't?" she asked.

The way he looked at her made goose bumps scatter over her. "Emily, most people can't."

"Oh," she said. She felt naked, though of course she had her pajamas on.

"You have a gift," Nate said earnestly. "An extremely cool, extremely unusual gift. It's called telepathy."

"Telepathy," Emily repeated.

"I researched it," Nate said.

"Because of me?"

"I wasn't sure it was real, but . . . well . . ."

Emily frowned. "And it's a gift? Are you sure? Because Mom says—"

"I know what Mom says, and I don't agree. Yes, it's a gift." Nate hesitated. "But Emily . . ."

"You think I shouldn't tell people," Emily finished. She slumped. "That if I do, they'll think I'm crazy, like Grandma Elnora."

"*No,*" Nate said. "I mean, yes about not telling people, but not the part about Grandma Elnora."

"I love Grandma Elnora," Emily said defensively.

"I do, too. I sometimes wonder if she messes with Mom on purpose, but I don't think she's crazy."

"But you think I should 'blend in,' like how Mom always says."

"That's not it," Nate said. "Or maybe it is, a little." He gazed at her. "Do you know what I want, Emily?"

She did, but she let him say the words. Anyway, her throat felt cloggy all of a sudden.

He found her foot with his, connecting them across the bed. "All I want is for you to be happy."

CHAPTER SIX

Ava

Ava went from Rocky's Diner to the apartment Mama shared with Aunt Elena. She let herself in through the unlatched screen door and heard Mama and Aunt Elena talking in the small living room. When Ava realized what they were talking about, she pressed herself against the kitchen wall and kept quiet.

"Klara, you can't go on like this forever," Aunt Elena said.

"I tried, Elena," Mama said. "You *know* I did."

"Only after I practically pushed you out the door. Come to think of it, I did push you out the door."

"Another woman was in my house, sitting at my

dining room table! What did you expect me to do?"

"Here's a thought," Aunt Elena said. "You could have marched into your house and claimed your dining room table. While you were at it, you could have claimed your husband! But no, you ran away like a child." She sighed. "Klara, you're not a child."

"If Emily didn't get to grow up, I shouldn't get to either," Mama said.

"For heaven's sake. You've *got* to be kidding me."

Ava heard the rustle of sofa cushions, followed by footsteps. Quickly, she opened the screen door and let it thump shut.

"Ava! You startled me!" said Aunt Elena, who held a plate sprinkled with cookie crumbs.

"Sorry," Ava said. "I came to talk to Mama."

Aunt Elena tilted her head toward the living room and said, "Go on in. Can I get you something to drink? A Coke?"

"Yes, please. Thanks."

Ava barely had time to greet her mother and sit down beside her before Aunt Elena returned with more cookies and Ava's Coke.

"This is a nice surprise," Aunt Elena said. "How's your day been going, Ava?"

For a few minutes, they made light chitchat. Aunt

Elena and Mama gave no indication that Ava had interrupted a strained conversation, and Ava was relieved to see that Mama was holding herself together. Mama *was* better than she'd been when she first returned to Willow Hill. She was better than she'd been even last month. Just, "better" wasn't enough.

Ava was surer than ever of the theory she'd proposed to her sisters. Mama was stuck. She didn't want to be, but she was like a fly trapped in amber, and the amber was her guilt about Emily. Ava renewed her determination to tug her free.

"Can we talk about Emily?" she asked abruptly.

Mama flinched. "What?"

With no time for the slow buildup, Ava turned to her aunt and said, "Aunt Elena, you're one of the people who says Emily never existed. But your expression sometimes . . ." Ava cocked her head. "Is that what you really and truly think?"

Aunt Elena's eyes flitted to Mama. Then she stared at her hands. "I don't share Vera's opinion that Klara made Emily up," she said carefully.

"What *is* your opinion?"

Aunt Elena hesitated, as if she were standing on a ledge trying to decide whether or not to leap. Then, in a tumble of words, she told Ava that although she

75

had no memory of Emily's existence, she *did* remember Mama confiding in her about her Wishing Day wish.

"Mama *told* you? She told you about the wish that erased Emily?!" Sparks zipped and zapped in Ava's brain cells. "Aunt Elena!"

"What . . . exactly . . . did I tell you, Elena?" Mama asked, her face ashen. "And when?"

Did Mama not remember, or was she testing Aunt Elena?

"You told me how guilty you felt," Aunt Elena said. "It was right after you made your wishes. *Immediately* after. You told me you'd promised Emily that the two of you would make your wishes together, but that you broke your promise and made your wishes alone."

Mama made a choked sound.

"Whoa," said Ava. "Go back. How could you and Emily have made your wishes *together*?"

"Emily and your mom had the same birthday," Aunt Elena explained. "That meant they had the same Wishing Day."

"Wait. What?!" Ava grabbed her hair by its roots. "What do you mean they had the same birthday? Why am I only hearing about this now?"

"Oh, Ava, millions of people share the same birthday," said Aunt Elena. "If you'd been born two days

76

earlier, you'd have had the same birthday as your mother, too."

True, Ava acknowledged. Mama's birthday was March thirteenth. Ava's was March fifteenth, referred to by people of her parents' generation as the ides of March. It was a Shakespeare thing.

Beware the ides of March! countless people had warned her gleefully.

You betcha! Ava was tempted to respond. *I mean, I'd have to know what the ides of March are in order to beware of them, but sure!*

"All right, fine," said Ava, bringing herself back on topic. Like a prosecutor grilling a witness on TV, she turned to Aunt Elena. She steepled her fingers. "Aunt Elena. Mama told you she'd promised to make her wishes with Emily, but she didn't."

"She and Emily were going to make them at sunrise on their Wishing Day, at the top of Willow Hill," Aunt Elena replied. "Instead, your mom made her wishes just past midnight, as soon as the fourteenth became the fifteenth."

"You came out of your bedroom just after I'd made them," Mama told Elena in a near whisper.

"I wanted a sip of water."

"I heard you in the hall. I opened my bedroom

77

door and beckoned you into my room. We . . . talked."

"You told me you'd messed up by making your wishes by yourself," Aunt Elena said. "You also told me . . . you know. About wishing you'd won that contest instead of Emily."

"That stupid, stupid contest." Mama stared at her lap. "And then, the next morning, it was just like I said, as if Emily had never existed. No one remembered her. No one except Elena—and even Elena didn't remember for long."

Aunt Elena's lips parted. She made as if to speak.

"What?" asked Ava.

Aunt Elena closed her mouth and shook her head.

Mama squeezed her hands between her thighs. "Everything was so awful. Everyone thought I was making stuff up! So I told Elena to forget everything I'd said. I *had* to." She met Aunt Elena's gaze, ashamed. "Over time, I convinced you that you'd made it all up—going to the bathroom, coming into my room, everything. You were young. You were easy to persuade."

"Slow down," Ava said. "Mama, you waited until just after midnight to make your wishes, right? Then you heard Aunt Elena in the hall, and the two of you talked, and you told her you regretted what you'd done."

78

Mama nodded miserably.

"But you were supposed to meet Emily at sunrise, at the top of Willow Hill. What happened with that?"

Mama's chin wobbled. "Elena went back to bed. I stayed awake. I waited until sunrise, and . . . I climbed to the top of Willow Hill."

"And?"

Tears welled in Mama's eyes. They spilled over and ran in rivulets down her cheeks. "I never set out to betray her!" She turned to Aunt Elena. "And unlike you, I could *never* forget Emily. I never *will* forget Emily!"

"Mama!" Ava said, her heart juddering.

"Klara?" said Aunt Elena. "I'm not the villain here. Neither are you."

"But I am!" Mama cried. "Of course I am!" She banged the coffee table with her fist, making the cups and plates jump.

Someone's cool fingers found Ava's. Gently, Aunt Elena squeezed Ava's hand.

"Everything changed," Mama said savagely. "Every day, all day long . . . my thoughts circled and lunged and bit. That's why I left Willow Hill, because I couldn't escape myself. Can you understand that, Ava?"

Ava nodded uncertainly. Before Mama left, she'd

written a letter to each of her daughters, instructing Papa to distribute them when each girl turned thirteen. Mama's letter to Natasha was richly detailed and apologetic. Her letter to Darya was pleading and melancholic. Ava had read them both, with her sisters' permission.

The letter Mama left for Ava, penned when Ava was only four, was . . . a dud. Ava felt bad for thinking that, but it was. Ava's letter was a weary farewell written to a four-year-old out of an exhausted sense of duty.

She can ask her sisters, Ava imagined Mama thinking as she completed the task of writing, folding, stuffing, envelope-licking. *Why repeat every painful detail?*

In all three of the letters to her daughters, Mama claimed that she didn't want to leave, but that she had no choice.

Except she did have a choice. Choices were everywhere. People made them every day.

When Mama left, she left us, Ava thought now. *Mama. Chose. That.*

On Aunt Elena's sofa, Mama fidgeted and drummed her fingers. "I promised myself I wouldn't return to Willow Hill until I was better," she said. "*Completely* better."

"Are you?" Ava asked.

Aunt Elena scolded her with a look.

Ava plunged on, even though it hurt. It all hurt so much. "When you left, were you trying to punish yourself?"

"I was. Yes."

"Were you trying to punish *us*?"

"No! Ava, never!"

Ava didn't respond. Mama could color it however she wanted, but Mama had disappeared, just like Emily. Only, Mama had disappeared on purpose.

"I can see how you would think that," Mama said. Her fingers curled on the tabletop, frail snails retreating into their shells. "But I wasn't in my right mind. I'm not sure I *have* a right mind anymore."

"Self-pity won't buy you a get-out-of-jail card," Aunt Elena said. "We've talked about this, Klara."

"But just as I couldn't let go of Emily, I couldn't even *begin* to let go of you, Ava," Mama continued. "You and your sisters. I missed you *so much*."

"And Papa?" Ava asked.

"And Papa," Mama said. She gestured at Aunt Elena, and then swept her hand in a broader arc. "And Elena and Vera. I missed you all. But I didn't *deserve* you. Don't you see?"

Ava's ribs tightened. She wanted to be done with blame. Not that she thought Mama was blameless! Mama had made a selfish wish. No way around it. Just, she'd been *thirteen*. Thirteen! Anyway, people made selfish wishes all the time. People did selfish things all the time. Even Emily herself must have thought and/or done selfish things at some point in her life!

Ava pressed her hand to her ribs, trying to ease the ache.

Emily.

Emily had paid the biggest price of all for Mama's actions.

Except nobody knows for sure that Emily existed, Ava reminded herself. *That means nobody knows for sure that she disappeared.*

"So why did you come back, Mama?" Ava asked slowly. "You didn't find Emily, so you didn't come home because of that. And you say you love us—"

"I *do* love you," Mama said.

"But you refuse to come back home, or talk to Papa." Ava held out her hands, palms up. "So why?"

A shadow crossed Mama's face. "I was pulled back. I can't explain it. Just, I woke up one morning and knew it was time."

"Natasha's wish," Ava said.

Mama nodded. "Yes. But I'm still . . . especially with your father, it's . . ."

"It's complicated for *all* of us, Mama," Ava implored.

Aunt Elena smoothed Ava's hair. "Your mother is worried that if she goes back to Nate, and then leaves *again* . . ."

"Why would she leave again?" Ava asked. "Mama, why would you leave again?"

"What if he's with this *Angela* woman?" said Mama. She threw back her head and groaned. "No, that's not it. Ava, it's just . . . it's Emily. Always Emily. What if the memories chase me away?"

Ava's skin tingled. All at once, everything in the living room grew sharper around the edges. The sun cut through the pale pink curtains. The light played over Mama's face, and for a microsecond, Ava could see her as she might be: a new person, different from who she'd been for so many pain-filled years.

"What if you found out the truth about Emily?" Ava asked. "The real truth?"

Mama grew still.

"What if Emily *is* safe and alive and . . . yeah," Ava went on. "Would you stop beating yourself up? Would you work things out with Papa, or at least try?"

"Ava, this isn't something to joke about," Mama said.

"Who says I'm joking?"

"Ava," said Aunt Elena. "Do you know something about Emily?"

Ava thought of Darya. She thought of Darya's friend Tally. She thought of the picture Tally drew, the picture Darya refused to acknowledge even though Darya'd been the one to find it.

She lifted her chin. "I do."

"What do you know?" Mama demanded, her voice raw.

"Okay, maybe I don't know *yet*," Ava said. "But I will. I promise."

Mama stood, her shin hitting the coffee table. "Do you know how many promises people make, Ava? Do you know how many promises people *break*?"

"I won't, though!" said Ava. "I—"

I promise. The word had been on her lips, so close to slipping out.

Mama squeezed past Aunt Elena. "I love you, Ava. I'm sorry I can't give you what you want from me. And I'm sorry"—she barked a laugh—"well, I'm sorry you can't give me what I want, either."

She strode from the living room, her breath coming

in gulps. "I'm just *sorry*, forever and ever sorry."

From the back of the apartment came the sound of a door being shut. Ava half-rose, but Aunt Elena put her hand on Ava's knee. Ava sat back down.

"Aunt Elena!" she exclaimed. "You're crying! Why are *you* crying?"

Aunt Elena reached for a napkin and blew her nose. She dabbed her eyes with the back of each hand. "Oh, Ava," she said, letting out a shuddering breath. "Your mom's not the only one with secrets."

I wish my sadness didn't make other people sad, too.

—Klara Blok, age thirty-six

CHAPTER SEVEN

Ava

"I don't want to burden you with more than you can handle," Aunt Elena said.

"Aunt Elena, I'm not a baby," said Ava.

Aunt Elena gave a small laugh, and Ava worried she'd sounded rude.

"I'm sorry," Ava said. "It's just, I'm the youngest person in my family, so everyone assumes I can't handle things. But I can."

"Of course you can—and believe me, I understand. *I'm* the baby of my family, you know."

"Yeah. Aunt Vera, then Mama, then you."

"I fought like crazy to make my sisters stop treating

me like a baby, and guess what?"

"What?"

She laughed again. "When they did, I missed it."

Well, I wouldn't, Ava wanted to say.

"It's hard being the youngest," Aunt Elena acknowledged. "It's hard being the middle sister, too. And the oldest." She paused. "There are advantages to each, as well."

"What made you cry?" Ava asked.

"I'll tell you, but humor me for a second. I'm your aunt. I get to pass along sage advice, don't I?"

Ava didn't want sage advice. She wanted to know Aunt Elena's secret.

"You, Ava, are your own self," Aunt Elena said. "You're obviously more than 'the baby' of the family. But, like it or not, you're also part of a whole."

"One of the Blok sisters, you mean?"

"You need Natasha and Darya, and they need you." Aunt Elena tucked a strand of hair behind Ava's ear. "You can resist being their baby sister, but would that change anything?"

"They could stop treating me like a baby," Ava said. "That would change things."

"Fair enough. I guess I'm saying . . . hmm. Don't let your desire not to be a certain way be the biggest factor that molds you into *you*."

"I already am me," Ava stated.

Aunt Elena laughed. It was a real laugh this time.

"What?"

"You made me think of your dad's mother, your grandma Rose. I only met her a few times, but according to your mom, she was quite set in her ways."

Ava cocked her head. "Please don't tell me I remind you of Grandma Rose."

"She put those horrid plastic slipcovers over the furniture in her living room," Aunt Elena said. "The *nice* furniture. The nice furniture that no one got to sit on."

"That's just how she is," Ava said defensively.

"Oh, honey, I know! But Klara always wondered if Nate's mom—your grandma Rose—became so rigid in response to her own mother's eccentricities."

"Great-Grandma Elnora," Ava said.

"You remember her?" Aunt Elena said.

"Only from stories. Enough to know that she'd never have used plastic slipcovers."

"Exactly."

"Are you saying that since Great-Grandma Elnora was anti–plastic slipcovers, that's why Grandma Rose loved them?" She took the thought further. Since

91

Great-Grandma Elnora believed in magic, was that why Grandma Rose hated it? Was that why Grandma Rose had flipped out when Ava pretended to sprinkle magic fairy dust over her bingo cards?

"Huh," Ava said. "So, if my knee-jerk reaction is to be the opposite of Natasha and Darya, then I'm still letting them say who I am, basically."

Aunt Elena looked surprised. "You are one smart young lady."

Ava tried not to be offended. "Thanks. I'm still not planning to use slipcovers, though. Now that that's settled, what secret are you keeping?"

Aunt Elena grew sober. She placed her hands flat against her thighs.

"Your mother thinks I forgot about Emily just like everyone else. She thinks that I . . ." She faltered. "That I remembered our middle-of-the-night discussion, but not the actual girl we discussed. Emily."

"Go on."

"The next morning, after Klara climbed Willow Hill, after Emily wasn't there to meet her, that was when everything got so messed up."

"I thought the Emily-disappearing part was when things got so messed up."

"Yes, just . . . let me tell this my own way." She

raked her hand through her hair. "Just as your mother never told anyone but me what she wished for, I've never told anybody—*any*body—what I'm about to tell you."

Yikes, Ava thought. Did she *want* to know?

"The next morning, at breakfast, everybody congratulated Klara on winning the Academic Olympiad," Aunt Elena said.

Ava nodded, digging her fingernails into her palms.

"Klara asked about Emily. Everyone said, 'What? Who?' Vera, my parents—they acted as if they had no idea who Klara was talking about." Aunt Elena looked as shaky as Ava felt. "I played along. I was confused. I was scared! If it was a practical joke, it made no sense. My parents weren't the sort of people to make practical jokes."

Aunt Elena glanced toward the back of the apartment. She lowered her voice. "Your mom pulled me away from the breakfast table. She dragged me into the kitchen and gripped me by the shoulders. She gripped me so hard."

"And?"

"'You remember her, don't you?' she said."

"My *mom* said that, to *you*," Ava clarified.

"When I didn't answer, she shook me and said,

'Elena. Do you remember Emily?' I did, and I admitted it. *But no one else did.* Not at school, not the waitresses at Rocky's, no one."

"Wait," Ava said. "Just ten minutes ago, with the cookies. We were all talking, and Mama said that you *didn't* remember Emily that next morning." Ava regarded her aunt. "Mama told you to *forget* what she'd said in the middle of the night."

"That evening, your mom pulled me into her room and shut the door," Aunt Elena said. "Her eyes, Ava. Her eyes were so wild. And she was thirteen. I was only ten! She said, 'We're the only ones. We're the only ones who remember her, Elena. What are we going to do?'"

Aunt Elena swiped at her eyes. "And I thought, '*We?* What are *we* going to do?' Because *I* didn't wish Emily away. *She* did!"

"She didn't 'wish Emily away,'" Ava said. "You know she didn't."

"Same difference," Aunt Elena said, and she sounded like a child.

Ava sat with it all. She stared at her aunt. She finally said, "You changed your story? Mama thinks she convinced you that you'd never had that conversation about Emily. But really, you convinced Mama that you'd forgotten Emily, just like everyone else?"

"It wasn't as if I could bring Emily back."

"You left Mama all alone."

"Klara left Emily all alone!"

"Did she? What does that even mean? Nobody has a clue what happened to Emily!"

Aunt Elena visibly made an effort to gather herself. "I *tried*. I told your mother I didn't remember Emily, yes. But I searched for Emily. I tried finding her father, your dad's dad who lives in California."

"Grandpa Dave."

"We didn't have the internet back then. There were phone books at the library, but California is a big state. Still, I found four hundred and fifty-seven listings for David, Dave, or D. Blok. It took time, but I called them all." She made a funny sound. "Oh, and we didn't have cell phones or data plans or any of that. I couldn't use my parents' phone. They'd see the calls on the bill. So I used pay phones, the most out-of-the-way ones I could find."

Ava saw a girl her own age—no, younger—enclosed in the glass box of an old-fashioned telephone booth. Ava had never seen a real telephone booth. In the picture in her mind, young Aunt Elena wore a dress like Laura Ingalls from the old TV show *Little House on the Prairie*, which Ava had seen reruns of. Young Aunt Elena wore her hair in plaits and rose on her toes in black lace-up boots, hooking her finger into the holes

95

of the rotary dial seven times, rotating the wheel to the stopping point, *swoosh*, before letting it return to starting position, click-*click-click-click-click*.

Actually, ten times, because of the California area code.

Actually, eleven times, because in the olden days, didn't people have to dial "1" before long-distance calls?

"It took me two years to call all those numbers," Aunt Elena said.

"What?! That's ridiculous!"

"No. Long-distance calls were expensive. On a weekday, it cost eighty cents to make a three-minute call to California. My allowance was two dollars a week. I earned money babysitting, and my mom could never understand where all that money went to." She gave a slight shake of her head. "Chewing gum. I told her I spent it on chewing gum."

"You didn't find him," Ava said flatly.

"I never reached a Dave Blok who was the father of Nate and Emily Blok, no," said Aunt Elena. "I couldn't rule out the possibility I'd missed him. People didn't always pick up. Some people never picked up. I could have dialed a wrong number . . ."

She faced Ava square on. "Your mom eventually

moved on, or pretended to. I was furious. The weight of knowing that a girl had *disappeared*, that because of my *sister*, a girl had disappeared . . . it crushed me. I started feeling as if *I* were going crazy. People said Klara was crazy; maybe I was, too. So, when it was finally my Wishing Day, do you know what I wished?"

Ava dealt out possibilities like playing cards: maybe Aunt Elena wished for Emily to come back, for everything to go back to normal, or for Klara not to have made that stupid wish about the contest in the first place. Maybe she wished she hadn't woken up that night, wanting a sip of water.

Ava discarded them all, because if Aunt Elena had made *any* of those wishes, she and Aunt Elena wouldn't be sitting here now. Mama wouldn't have shut herself up in her bedroom. There wouldn't be an Angela in Papa's life.

"I wished to forget Emily too," Aunt Elena said softly. "That was the wish I could make come true myself, and I suppose I did." With her eyes, she begged Ava to understand. "Denial is a powerful force."

Ava was dumbfounded. She understood that Aunt Elena was hurting, and she didn't want to dig a knife into her wound or whatever. And yet, seriously?!

Ava snapped a sugar cookie in half. She snapped

one of the halves in half.

"So now, when you think of Emily . . . ," Ava began.

"I didn't, not for years and years," Aunt Elena said. "But after Natasha's Wishing Day, bits started creeping back. After Darya's birthday, more crept back. You girls, with all your questions. And your mother! She can't go a day without mentioning Emily!"

"So now that you remember her again, why don't you tell people?"

"Because I *don't* remember her again!" Aunt Elena exploded. She pressed her lips together and shot a look down the hall. "I remember the events that happened, but I remember them the way I'd remember the plot of a play. Act One: Klara made a wish. Klara told me her wish. Her wish made a girl named Emily disappear."

She leaned forward, holding her head with her fingertips. "Act Two. I searched for the girl named Emily. I found no trace of her. So, on my Wishing Day, I wished to no longer remember her." She peered at Ava through the hair falling into her eyes. "The end."

"I hate that play," Ava said.

"Yes. You're not the only one."

"Shouldn't there be an Act Three?"

Aunt Elena moved her hand to suggest it was out of her control, and Ava felt a surge of frustration.

"You're acting as if . . . as if it were a play *for real*, and you're just doing what the script says to do!" she said.

Aunt Elena lifted her head. "What an odd thing to say, Ava." Something was going on with her features, some internal battle playing out that sent a shiver up Ava's spine. "What a very. Odd. Thing to *say*."

"Is there anything about any of this that *isn't* odd?" Ava demanded.

Aunt Elena shook her head. It seemed as though she had one foot planted in the world in front of them, the *now* world, and the other foot planted in another place, another *when*.

"Is there any way you can prove what you've told me?" asked Ava.

"About Emily? No."

"And there's no one who can confirm your version of things, since I'm the only person you've told your story to."

"I'm afraid you're right," said Aunt Elena. She frowned. "Unless . . ."

"Unless what?"

"There is something. It might matter, or it might not."

"About Emily?"

"I can't grab hold of it," said Aunt Elena.

"Is it about Mama?"

"No, I don't *think* so . . ."

"Then what?"

"You asked if there was anyone who could confirm my story," Aunt Elena said. "I said no, but I think there might be, after all. It's . . . it's like a toothache, but in my mind. It's there. I just can't get to it!"

Ava got a crazy idea. An absolutely ridiculous idea. She took Aunt Elena's hands and said, "Did you know that scientists, lots of them, think telepathy is real?"

Aunt Elena looked bewildered.

"Telepathy," Ava repeated. "The ability to read another person's thoughts."

"I know what it is," said Aunt Elena.

"Scientists also say that more people have it than maybe we know. That a person could be telepathic and not even know it!"

Aunt Elena's smile was fond, if amused. She returned to Ava, present again and no longer in the world-between-worlds she'd seemed trapped in. "Do you want to try and read my mind, sweet niece?" She spread her arms, flopped against the sofa, and closed her eyes. "Go for it."

Ava set her shoulders. She had no clue what she was doing, but the papers she'd read mentioned focus, concentration, and single-mindedness of purpose, so . . . okay. She closed her eyes and mentally reached out to Aunt Elena.

Jellyfish tentacles, she thought, imagining slender tendrils floating from her mind to her aunt's. Then she thought, *No! Yuck!* She didn't want jellyfish tentacles connecting them. Jellyfish were pretty, but they stung people.

She tried again. She imagined probes. Pleasant, well-intentioned probes, *not* UFO-abduction-story probes. She imagined electrodes, but without the skullcaps. She imagined energy from her mind seeking energy from Aunt Elena's mind, and for a moment, she felt something! A door, edging open. Brilliant light seeping through the crack, tiny wings fluttering and surrounding Ava with Aunt Elena-ness . . .

And then, gone.

Calm. Neutral. A door merging seamlessly with a wall, a lake without ripples.

"You can open your eyes, Aunt Elena."

Aunt Elena did. "Nothing?"

"Nothing." Ava tried to hide her disappointment.

"Well, it was worth a try," Aunt Elena said. "Don't feel bad." She stood and took the cookie plate into the kitchen.

Ava trailed behind her and put her Coke can in the

recycling bin. "So . . . guess I'll take off."

"It was good to see you," Aunt Elena said. "Come anytime. And Ava?"

Ava paused.

"Don't ever stop trying. Even if it seems silly, even if it seems pointless—never give up hope."

"Okay."

Aunt Elena adopted an I'm-about-to-quote-something expression. Speaking clearly, she said, "'Hope is the thing with feathers— / that perches in the soul— / and sings the tune without the words— / and never stops—at all.'"

She smiled sadly. "That's one of your mom's favorite poems. It's by Emily Dickinson."

"It's . . . nice," Ava said.

"Who knows?" Aunt Elena continued. "Maybe there will be an Act Three in this play we seem stuck in. We can hope, can't we?"

Ava opened the back door. "Yeah, sure," she said. "We can all sprout feathers and hope."

Aunt Elena clapped her hand over her mouth.

"What?" Ava said.

Aunt Elena dropped her hand. "Yes! That!"

"Huh?"

"I don't know how I forgot. I can't *believe* I forgot!

But just now, it came to me out of nowhere!"

"Aunt Elena—"

"The Bird Lady! I was in the woods by the lake, and she called to me from her hideaway in the forest. Do you know the spot I mean? In the trunk of the huge oak?"

Ava knew nothing about a forest hideaway.

"She was looking for me," Aunt Elena continued. "It was my Wishing Day, and the Bird Lady was looking for me because . . ." Wonder illuminated Aunt Elena's face. "*She* told me what to wish for!"

Sometimes, for no apparent reason, Ava's fingertips grew numb. That happened now.

"She knew I was unhappy," said Aunt Elena. "She called me over, and I went to her, and she said, 'You're quite troubled, Elena Kosrov, but you needn't be.' *Needn't*. Such an archaic word." Her gaze went distant. "She told me I should wish to forget Emily."

"I don't understand."

"There was a *bird* in her hair, and another on her shoulder. How could I have forgotten?"

Ava experienced the sensation of falling. Or of flying?

"*The Bird Lady told me to forget Emily,*" Aunt Elena said again. She looked at Ava intently. "If you

103

can get her to admit it, you'll have the evidence you're looking for."

Ava swallowed twice before she could speak. "Thanks, Aunt Elena. Will you say bye to Mama for me?"

She didn't wait for an answer, just hurried out of Aunt Elena's apartment and headed for the forest.

CHAPTER EIGHT

Emily, age eleven

By the summer before sixth grade, Emily's dad had taken to sleeping on the sofa every night. It was awful. Sometimes, Emily slept downstairs with him, on a sleeping bag on the floor. Emily suspected Nate wanted to as well, but felt like he was too old. Or maybe he didn't want to upset their mother.

"You're enabling your father to leave this family!" Emily's mom told Emily. "You should be punishing him instead. If you let him sleep downstairs alone—if we all leave him down there alone—he'll return to the upstairs bedroom, where he belongs."

Emily knew that secretly, her mom wanted to

punish *her*. One afternoon, Emily looked up from a sketch she was working on and caught her mom staring at her with slitted eyes.

You, her mom thought. *If only you—*

Then those thoughts blanked out, as if a lid had been slammed down. Sometimes her mom did want to punish Emily, but she was never proud of herself when she thought such things.

It's not Emily's fault, Rose, her mom told herself. *If Dave would just support me when I need him to, instead of arguing with me about everything!*

Except her parents didn't argue about "everything." They argued about Emily. It gave Emily a stomachache.

"Can I see your drawing?" her mom asked, approaching Emily with red-rimmed eyes.

Warily, Emily tilted her sketch pad.

"The willow tree," her mom said. Her voice faltered. "It's lovely."

"It's okay, Mom," Emily said. The town associated the willow tree with magic, and since her mom hated magic, Emily knew she wasn't a fan of the willow. "You don't have to like it. It's not, like, the law or anything."

Her mom's eyes welled with tears, and she stalked

away. They both tried to reach out to each other, and they both failed, again and again. Were some daughters simply not meant to be born to certain mothers?

No. Emily didn't accept that. One far-off day in the future, if Emily was a mom, she'd make sure she did right by her daughter. If she had a daughter.

Tension continued to grow between her parents, and Emily, like most kids in her situation, knew the "talk" was coming. The divorce talk. She *knew* it was coming, yet when it did, it nevertheless sucked the air out of the room.

"It's nobody's fault," said her mother.

"Nate? Emily? You'll always come first," said her father.

And, each in his and her awkward way, used empty sentences to explain that they'd grown apart from each other, that's all.

The worst part was when Nate cried.

Emily wanted to cry, but she felt numb inside. Her parents' claim that they grew apart from each other was true. They didn't laugh anymore. Their conversations were strained. But if Emily wasn't in the picture . . .

Her mom wanted to change Emily, to increase her chances of blending in with kids who colored within the lines. Her dad wanted Emily to be who she was, and to feel good about who she was. But how could she? If she was different—normal—her parents wouldn't have been at odds with each other.

In August, her dad took a job all the way across the country.

"California," he said the day he loaded up the U-Haul. "In California, oranges grow in people's backyards. When you kids visit, you can have fresh-squeezed orange juice whenever you want. It'll be great!"

"I wouldn't count on it," her mother said. "Nothing will ever be great again."

"Rose . . . ," Emily's dad said.

Emily went to her dad and hugged him. She smelled his aftershave. She smelled his sweat, which was tangy. "Take me with you," she whispered.

"What's that, honey?" her dad said.

"Nothing," she mumbled.

She and Nate stood at the end of the driveway and waved until he was out of sight. Behind them, their mom closed the front door with a bang.

At school, she felt pity radiating from the teachers and some of the kids. Curiosity, too. Several times she caught Klara Kosrov gazing at her, and for no reason, it made her mad.

She reminded herself that Klara Kosrov had always been one of the nice girls in her grade. She still felt unnerved, so she reached out to test Klara's thoughts.

At once, she felt Jell-O-y in her knees.

Klara *did* feel bad for Emily, like the other kids. But not in a self-righteous way or a *tsk-tsk* way. Klara felt bad in a sad way.

Klara wanted to reach out to her, Emily could tell. Twice, Klara almost said something. The third time she tried to work up her nerve, Emily took pity on her, offering up a melancholy smile.

"Hi," Klara said, stepping closer. She twirled a strand of her dark hair around her finger. "I, um, heard about your parents. I don't want to say anything dumb like 'it'll all be fine' or 'it's better for them to be happy, even if it means they're apart.' Because what do I know? My parents aren't divorced."

Klara smacked her palm to her forehead. "That came out wrong. Omigosh, that's not what I meant to say."

"It's all right," said Emily.

Klara's hand went to her hair again, pushing it past her ear so that it spilled in a glossy waterfall over her shoulder. "I'm just sorry. It must really suck."

"Yeah," Emily said.

Another sixth grader, Holly Newcomb, wasn't nearly so kind. Holly was new to Willow Hill. She wore black eyeliner and ironic plaid skirts.

"Did your parents tell you it wasn't your fault?" Holly said, accosting Emily during PE.

"Excuse me?" said Emily.

"If they did, they lied," Holly said.

Emily paused before speaking. She sensed Holly's deep loneliness. She sensed Holly's need to make someone else feel bad in a desperate attempt to make herself feel better.

"I can tell you're upset about something," Emily said carefully, doing her best to channel Klara's generosity. "Do you, um, want to talk about it?"

Holly drew back. She called Emily a word that rhymed with "witch," spun on her heel, and didn't speak to Emily again.

I wish for no more pimples.

—VERA KOSROV, AGE THIRTEEN

CHAPTER NINE

Ava

Ava strode through the woods near City Park, craning her neck to look for what Aunt Elena had called the Bird Lady's hideaway. She'd said something about a huge oak tree, but Ava wasn't positive what an oak tree looked like. Oak *wood*, she could recognize from Papa's shop. But the tree itself?

She knew maple leaves. So pretty, like stars or outstretched fingers. She knew sarsaparilla, because Papa had taught her that its stem was good to chew on. A sarsaparilla leaf looked like a ghost, a friendly, cartoon ghost with a large round head and two up-stretched arms.

But oak. Oak, oak, oak. She knew a song about an oak tree. She'd learned it in preschool. It had to do with . . . oh! Little acorns growing into big oaks!

Well, *acorns*, sure. She shifted her perspective, scanning the ground instead of the sky.

"Over here, pet," called a voice.

Ava froze. Then, slowly, she lifted her head and turned in the direction of the voice.

"Well done, pet!" exclaimed the Bird Lady.

Ava's heart pitter-pattered beneath her T-shirt, but she wasn't scared, exactly. Startled? Yes. But the Bird Lady looked kind, just as Ava remembered. Her voice was old, but not croaky, not witchy. Certainly not wicked-witch witchy, as in, "I'll get you, my pretty— and your little dog, too!"

"I was looking for you," Ava said.

"And I for you, Ava Blok," replied the Bird Lady. "Or rather, I was *waiting* for you."

The Bird Lady stepped out of the shadows. She wore overalls and a faded plaid shirt. Her gray hair looked as soft as dandelion fluff—and was there a bird nestled within?

There was: a brown sparrow with bright, curious eyes. Warmth spread through Ava, a shimmering, golden appreciation for the wonders of the world.

The Bird Lady beckoned Ava forward, indicating a tree several feet away. "Come. It's lovely, you'll see."

Ava went to the tree—the *oak* (the ground around it was sprinkled with acorns)—and touched its rough bark.

Its roots were thicker than Ava's thighs, and a mass of vines clambered clockwise around its trunk, reaching twenty feet high and extending along the uppermost branches. Purple tendrils drooped from the vines, reminding Ava of the feather boas she used to sling around her neck when she was playing dress-up.

"Blue Moon wisteria," the Bird Lady said, stroking one of the tendrils.

"But it's purple, not blue."

"Not in the moonlight," the Bird Lady said.

Ava circled the oak, trailing her finger along the wisteria blossoms. Several times, Ava caught the Bird Lady sneaking peeks at her. Ava stopped midway around the massive trunk, feeling an urge to dig into the soil and unearth what lay beneath.

May I? she asked the Bird Lady with a lift of her eyebrows.

You may, the Bird Lady replied, dipping her head.

The Bird Lady's gesture was queenly, stirring something deep within Ava. She thought of ancient times and ancient ways. She thought of ancient rituals, possibly brought to Willow Hill from Russia, where Ava's ancestors hailed from and which Mama and her aunts called the old country. Legend had it that it was one of Ava's ancestors, a great-great-many-times-great-grandmother from Mama's side, who had brought magic from the old country to their small town of Willow Hill.

It could be true, Ava thought. When she was a child, she'd been entranced by the legend. As she'd grown older, she'd talked herself into dismissing it, especially after Grandma Rose had scolded Ava for living in "a fantasy world." Grandma Rose had tutted and quoted a Bible verse at her: "When I was a child, I spoke as a child, I understood as a child, I thought as a child. But when I grew up, I put away childish things."

The verse had hit home. Ava did not want to be a child.

Yet now, standing with the Bird Lady in the heart of the forest, a timeless feeling seeped into Ava's pores. The past, the present, the future . . .

Ava sucked in her breath: all of life was one long moment!

The revelation dazzled her.

She blinked and came back to herself. She kicked at the soil with the toe of her sneaker, uncovering a gnarled root. It looked no different from the other roots, but something about it tugged at her.

She glanced at the Bird Lady, and the Bird Lady swept the wisteria vines to the side, revealing a large, dark hollow within the trunk of the oak.

"Whoa!" said Ava.

The Bird Lady smiled more broadly. "I know."

The hollow was big enough for a person to duck into. To sit, to hide. "It's fantastic."

"It's where I store my secrets."

Secrets! Yes! At once, Ava remembered why she'd come. "My aunt. Aunt Elena. When she was my age, you told her to wish to forget Emily!"

A shadow crossed the Bird Lady's face. She bade Ava to step into the oak's hidden nook, and Ava did. Within the hollow, wedged into nooks and crannies, Ava spotted dozens of glass soda bottles. More bottles hung from the roof of the hollow. The bottles dangled from lengths of twine, one end of the twine looped around the bottle's neck and the other end secured to one of the many knobby bits in the upper reaches of the trunk.

Within each glass bottle was a rolled-up scroll of paper.

"What are these?" Ava asked.

"My secrets, as I said."

Ava reached for one.

"*No,*" the Bird Lady said. Ava withdrew her hand.

Unsure what to do, she lowered herself to the moist soil. Bark dug into Ava's back, and she shifted positions, drawing her knees to her chest and holding them with her arms. The Bird Lady mimicked Ava's posture. The space was so tight, their knees touched.

Ava's memory flashed to an earlier time. She'd been little, maybe four years old, and she and Mama were playing house in a pink plastic cottage that belonged to Ava's preschool. At noon, after school was dismissed and the other parents and children went home, Mama and Ava sometimes snuck back into the playground. Laughing and holding hands, they'd dash to the child-sized cottage with its stools shaped like red mushrooms with white polka dots. Mama had to scrunch to perch on one, and even so, her head grazed the cottage ceiling.

"Tea?" Ava would ask.

"Oh, yes," Mama would say. "And biscuits, if you please."

In England, cookies were called biscuits. Mama had taught Ava that, and Ava had been charmed. When they sipped their pretend tea, they'd lifted their little fingers.

Ava, at four, hadn't understood her mother's depression, just that on some days, Papa or one of her aunts picked her up from preschool instead of Mama. "Your mother is tired," Ava was told, or "Your mother had a rough day." Ava had no premonition that one day Mama would be gone. Not resting, not having a rough day, just gone.

"Hold on," Ava said, giving herself a shake. She was sitting knees-to-knees with the Bird Lady, not Mama. "How did you know my name?"

"How did you know mine?" the Bird Lady retorted.

"I don't. I mean, obviously 'the Bird Lady' isn't your *real* name. What is?"

The Bird Lady's eyes darted away. She picked at an imaginary bit of fluff on her overalls.

"Fine," Ava said. She wasn't here for games. "You said you were waiting for me. Why?"

"I imagine it's the same reason you came looking for me."

"My aunt said you knew Emily."

"I did. I hope to again one day."

"You do? Meaning what?"

"Meaning exactly what I said: that I hope to know her again one day."

"So she existed? For real?"

The Bird Lady huffed. "Of course she did! Hopefully, she still does!"

"Will you tell me about her? Please?"

The Bird Lady didn't answer.

Ava picked up a leaf, damp and beginning to rot. She shredded it into strips.

"I knew your mother, too," the Bird Lady said. *"Klara."*

Ava stopped.

"Emily and Klara, they had such big plans," the Bird Lady said.

"For their Wishing Days," said Ava. Only moments ago, she'd assured the Bird Lady that she had no doubts Emily was real, but she'd said that to make sure the Bird Lady kept talking. Also, Ava had always *wanted* Emily to be real, because she wanted to believe her mother. The story about Emily was horrible, but the story without Emily was worse. If Emily didn't exist, and never had existed, then Mama hadn't abandoned their family out of grief and guilt. She'd just . . . abandoned them.

But now, listening to the Bird Lady—hearing the wistfulness and the regret in the Bird Lady's voice— Ava realized she'd turned a corner.

Emily *was* real.

Emily was *real*.

Emily. Was. Real.

"She and Klara had planned to meet at the top of Willow Hill at sunrise and make their wishes together," the Bird Lady said. "But Klara failed. Klara broke their promise, and Emily suffered the consequences."

"But it was an accident," Ava said.

"Your mother wanted to be special," the Bird Lady said.

Ava bristled.

"As for Emily, she *was* special," the Bird Lady went on. "She was an artist, a good artist, and one day she'd be famous. Everyone said so."

"So why did you tell my aunt to forget all about her? *Did* you tell Aunt Elena that?"

The Bird Lady jiggled her knee. "Do you want me to continue?"

"If you don't deny it, I'll assume you did."

"Assume what you please. If you want to hear from me what I may or may not have told Elena, however, I suggest you shut up."

Ava set her jaw.

"Klara was special, too," the Bird Lady said, giving Ava a reproving look. "Of course she was. I'm just . . . I'm hoping you'll understand."

"Understand what?"

"*Klara* didn't think she was special," the Bird Lady continued. "That was the problem. She was popular, she was pretty, but she wanted more."

"Well, I think that's a good thing," Ava said. She was proud of Mama for not caring about superficial qualities.

"There's something else," the Bird Lady said. "That silly contest. The Academic Olympiad." The Bird Lady pursed her lips. "Emily didn't care whether she won or not. For Emily, art was about creation. About adding beauty to the world."

Ava got a bad feeling in her stomach.

"And then there was Nate," said the Bird Lady.

"Papa," whispered Ava.

"Your papa, yes. Also Emily's older brother. Klara knew he was the one for her from the first time she met him." Color bloomed on the Bird Lady's cheeks. "She wanted to impress him, that's all! She never meant . . . *I* never meant . . . nobody ever meant for Emily to disappear!"

Ava felt queasy. The nook in the tree wasn't cozy. It was claustrophobic. Not enough air. She tried to rise, but the Bird Lady pressed down on her leg.

"It's not easy for me, either, pet," she said, and to Ava's horror, fat glossy tears welled in the Bird Lady's eyes.

"What am I supposed to 'understand'?" Ava asked. "What haven't you told me?"

The Bird Lady lifted her chin. "Natasha and Darya did their part. You should be proud of them. You should be proud of yourself as well." She nodded and sniffled. "You're starlings, all three of you."

"Starlings?"

The Bird Lady gave a quivery laugh. "Darlings. You're all *darlings*."

The wisteria draping from the oak tree rustled, and Ava heard the flapping of wings. Three birds swooped past the entrance of the nook.

"Ava!" they cried. "Ava, Ava, Ava!"

Ava's breath caught. She stretched forward, straining to see past the flowering vines. "Did . . . did that just happen?"

The Bird Lady gazed at Ava. "It's up to you to finish what your sisters started. I think you know that already."

"What do you hope I'll understand?" Ava whispered.

"It concerns your mother. But before I tell your mother's story, I need to tell my own," the Bird Lady said. "They're . . . connected."

"And Emily, and Aunt Elena?"

"We're all connected." She spread her arms. "Everyone, everything, and if one piece is knocked out of place . . ."

"Someone has to set it right," Ava finished.

The Bird Lady nodded. Her eyes were still shiny. "Here we go, then. I'll get to it as best I can."

Ava waited.

"We don't have much time, you see."

Ava waited.

The Bird Lady sucked in a breath of air, then blew it out.

Ava started to speak, but didn't. A quiet sort of calm spread through her body. She shifted positions within the cramped space, sitting criss-cross applesauce and brushing a twig from under her bottom.

She folded her hands in her lap and waited.

I wish, just sometimes, that people could know what I was thinking, without my saying a word.

—EMILY BLOK, AGE TWELVE

CHAPTER TEN

Emily, age thirteen

On Emily's thirteenth birthday, Emily, Nate, and their mom had a special birthday breakfast, meaning that the three of them sat at the table and ate their cereal together. Nate plucked the colorful marshmallows from his bowl of Lucky Charms and gave them to Emily. He also gave her a clumsily wrapped box of colored pencils. Good ones, from the art store.

"Nate, thank you," Emily said, already in love with the pencils in their perfectly aligned spectrum of colors.

Her mom gave Emily a pink blouse made from a flowy fabric that looked silky but felt scratchy. It had capped sleeves. A loopy bow hung from the collar.

"It's exactly like the one that nice Maggie Stanton has," her mom proclaimed.

Maggie Stanton, whose parents gave her a kitten in the third grade. The kitten would be a cat now. Had Maggie named it Mittens? Emily wondered.

"I saw Marjory and Maggie having a mother-daughter tea, and Maggie was wearing a carbon copy of this blouse, only in pale blue. They were going to get their nails done afterward. Doesn't that sound fun? Would you like to get a manicure together, sweetheart?"

"Um, sure?" Emily said.

Her mother beamed, and Emily felt a stab of guilt. If agreeing to a manicure was all it took to make her mother happy, she should do it more often.

Emily headed for her bedroom after putting her bowl and spoon in the dishwasher. Her mom called her back and placed a box on the counter. Her lips twitched. She said, "It's from your father."

Emily's eyes flew to the return address: California, where oranges grew in people's backyards. Maybe in her father's backyard. Emily didn't know. She and Nate had yet to visit. Their dad had extended dozens of invitations, volunteering to pay for their plane tickets, but their mom always came up with reasons to say no. The timing was bad. They'd miss too many school days. There was a chance that the kids' long-lost uncle might pop by for the weekend, no matter the weekend.

Sometimes Emily wondered if her mom was holding them hostage to punish their dad.

No. Emily *knew* that her mom was holding them hostage to punish their dad.

"Aren't you going to open it?" her mom asked.

Emily would have preferred to open it alone, but felt helpless against the force of her mother's curiosity. Her parents had been divorced for two years, her mother refused to let Emily and Nate see their dad, and yet she grasped for any detail, large or small, about Emily's dad's new life . . . and his new wife. Especially his new wife.

Emily opened the box and pulled out a soft white throw pillow with a unicorn on it. Her heart lifted, then fell. She liked the pillow. She did. Just, last year— twelve months ago, and no more—she would have *loved* it.

Emily was growing older. Her dad no longer knew her as well as he used to.

"How cute," her mother said, peering over Emily's shoulder. "Is there anything else? A card?"

Emily upended the box, and a card slid out. On the front was a potato wearing a party hat. Beneath the potato were the words, "This is the day you've been waiting for . . ."—and inside the card—". . . since you were a tot! Congratulations! You're officially a teenager!"

Ah, Emily thought, getting the pun. *No longer a tater tot.* Melancholy washed over her, pale and familiar.

Happy birthday, kiddo, her father had written in his slanted penmanship. *Blaine and I wish we could celebrate with you. Remember, our doors are always open. Say the word and I'll arrange a plane ticket. Same for Nate. Say hi to him for us. We miss you both.*

Blaine, the stepmother Emily had never met.

Have a great day, and may all your wishes come true, said the last bit. *Love, Dad.*

Emily's mother held out her hand. "May I?"

Emily shut the card. "He said happy birthday, that's all." She turned to Nate. "And to tell you hi."

"He'll call this evening, I suppose," Emily's mom said. "Remember to tell him about your school fees for this semester. He needs to pay half. It's his responsibility."

"He sent the check in January," said Emily.

Her mom huffed. "Oh, did he? That man." She

tapped her lips, then rolled her eyes elaborately. "That's right. He sent it in one of those legal-sized envelopes, all business, not even a note asking how we're doing. One little note—is that too much to ask?"

Emily and Nate exchanged a quick glance. They talked on the phone with their father once a month. He *did* ask how they were doing.

"All right, back to the day," her mother said, all sudden efficiency. "I know we'd planned to visit your grandmother at the care center this afternoon, but one of the aides called and told me she's having one of her tired spells. Just wants to sleep and watch her soap operas." Her mom's eyes slid away. She'd received no such call, and Emily knew it. "We'll go see her next weekend. It's not as if she'll know the difference."

Emily escaped to her bedroom with her card and unicorn pillow. She loved her odd grandmom Elnora, who would most certainly realize they failed to visit her on Emily's thirteenth birthday. Thirteenth birthdays were a big deal in Willow Hill, such a big deal that Emily knew that's why her mom had canceled the visit. Her mom didn't want Grandmom Elnora talking to Emily about her favorite topic: magic.

Not for the first time, or the hundredth, Emily vowed that if she ever had a child, she would be a different sort of mother from her own. She would try and see her child with clear eyes. To be the right sort of mother for the child she was given, whatever kind of child she or he was.

Emily had a vision so powerful it knocked the breath out of her: she was in a pool of water, staring up through murky water. First, she experienced the vision as if it were actually happening, as if she were in her body, watching the water close over her as she was swallowed by the depths. Then she saw her body from above, as if she were looking down at herself. She saw her dark eyes widen and her pale face sink deeper and deeper.

She came out of it with a jolt, dizzy and nauseated. Sweat beaded on her forehead. She sucked in sweet clean air.

What had just happened?

She'd had moments of déjà vu before, half memories that slipped out of her grasp like silverfish. But this . . .

She'd remembered herself drowning, although there'd been no thrashing or gasping for air. She hadn't fought the submersion. She'd just sunk.

At once, she felt horribly itchy. *Twitchy*, like spiders were crawling down her back. Like someone had walked over her grave.

"Get it together," she muttered under her breath. This was her birthday. She refused to spend it moping around, so she grabbed her art pad and her new pencils and headed to City Park Lake.

Outside, a breeze blew strands of hair into her face. She pulled an elastic off her wrist, gathered her hair into a bunch and pulled it through the elastic. She twisted the elastic and did the same thing again, repeating the pattern until she was left with a tight ponytail. The process satisfied her, familiar and routine.

Halfway to the park, she saw two girls roller-skating along the sidewalk, arms wobbling as they fought to keep their balance. They were probably nine or ten, and she thought one of them looked like Elena Kosrov, Klara Kosrov's little sister. Klara and Emily shared a birthday, which meant that Klara'd turned thirteen today, too. All through elementary school, Emily and Klara had brought treats for the other kids on the same day. Klara's had always been better, because they were homemade.

Emily paused to watch Elena and her friend. Emily used to love roller-skating, though she'd roller-skated solo. She was swept into a there-and-then-gone recollection of the exhilaration of zooming down a steep hill, sometimes going so fast she had to dive into the bushes bordering a driveway to bring herself to a stop.

Elena and her friend laughed wildly, and their happiness lifted Emily's spirits.

CHAPTER ELEVEN

Ava

"I always felt awkward as a girl," the Bird Lady finally said. "Always out of place."

Wind stirred the wisteria vines dangling from the oak tree. The outside world was still there, Ava reminded herself. Her sisters, her aunts, Mama and Papa—they were doing whatever they were doing beyond the loamy expanse of the forest.

The curtain of purple wisteria blooms *seemed* to separate the tree hollow from reality, yes.

But it doesn't really, Ava reassured herself.

The Bird Lady leaned close. "I just . . . I never was able to understand how other people functioned in the world. I would laugh when others didn't, for example. And things other people found funny, I didn't understand. I always thought there must be a rule book I was missing."

"You were the odd girl out," Ava said.

The Bird Lady pointed at her. "Exactly, and an odd *duck* as well." She tutted. "But I didn't want to be an odd duck. Heavens, no. Girls in my grade, girls I'd gone to school with for years, they didn't even know my name!"

"What *is* your name?" asked Ava.

"And so, as my Wishing Day approached—this was eons ago—I concluded that if I could simply see the world as others saw it, I could unlock the secret. Learn the rules. Be . . . well . . . normal. Popular."

The Bird Lady blinked. "And then my poor mother . . . Well, she died soon after my thirteenth birthday." She checked to see if Ava was paying attention. "She died *after* my birthday, but *before* my Wishing Day. Before she died, she gave me one last bit of advice—she *was* a good mother, the best!—but I failed to heed it."

Ava was intrigued, but impatient. The Bird Lady's speech felt rehearsed. Perhaps it was. If, as the Bird Lady said, there was a task that her sisters had started, and that Ava needed to finish, maybe the Bird Lady had put together a few words for the occasion.

The Bird Lady dabbed at her eyes. "Mothers. Can't live with them; can't live without them. Am I right?"

"No," Ava said, her tone leaving no room for doubt. There was a middle road, and Ava planned on finding it. "So, what did you wish for, on your Wishing Day?"

"Oh, well . . . *things*," said the Bird Lady. She gave Ava a meaningful look.

"Things?"

"One thing, really. For my first wish, I wished for one specific thing. Do you want to know what it was?"

"Um, yes. Please."

"Then ask!"

"Seriously? I already did."

"You have to ask me *specifically*, about *the one specific thing*."

Ava felt as if she were in a mixed-up version of Rumpelstiltskin or some other upside-down fairy tale. "*Ok-a-a-a-y*. What was the one specific thing you wished for on your Wishing Day?"

"Not like that. You have to ask . . . better," the Bird Lady said. She gave Ava another meaningful look. She waggled her eyebrows up and down.

"Better how?"

"Oh dear. You're not the brightest lightbulb in the lightbulb shop, are you?"

"*You're* not the brightest . . . question asker!" Ava retorted.

"We do the best with what we have," the Bird Lady muttered to herself. She took a breath. "When you look through a window, what do you see?"

"Whatever's past the windowpane," Ava said.

"Yes! But, humans. Do humans have windows?"

"In their houses, they do."

"Yes, I suppose. But do humans themselves have windows? Hmm?"

Ava held her hands up. "No. Humans do not have windows."

"Oh, for pity's sake. True, humans don't have windows, not literally. But a poetic sort of person might say that a certain part of a human is *similar* to a window."

"A person's eyes, then," Ava said, mystified. "'Eyes are the window to the soul.' So?"

"Yes! Good girl!" The Bird Lady clapped. "Now, ask again—what I wished for!"

"For eyes that were windows to your soul?"

"Don't be obtuse!" the Bird Lady said. "I didn't want people to see *my* soul. I had no interest in that.

What I wanted was to see . . ." She rolled her hand, encouraging Ava to finish the thought.

Ava felt as if she'd been thrust onto a game show without being told the rules. "Other people's souls? By looking into their eyes?"

The Bird Lady turned pink. "Close, so very close! Ask me one more time what I wished for, darling girl! And use a full sentence. Start with, 'For your first wish, your impossible wish, did you wish for . . . ?' And go on from there."

Ava didn't like it, but she went along with it. "Fine. For your first wish, your impossible wish, did you wish that you could look into people's eyes and"—she pushed through—"see their souls?"

The Bird Lady seemed incapable of speech, but she grabbed Ava's hands and squeezed them, nodding rapidly.

"You wished to look into a person's eyes and see her *soul*?" Ava repeated. "Why? And what would that even mean?"

The Bird Lady cleared her throat. It took several attempts before she could answer. "Within a girl's soul lives everything that makes her *her*. Her fears, her dreams, her secrets. What makes her happy. What makes her sad."

"So, basically, you wanted total omniscience," Ava said.

"I wanted it all, yes."

Ava's skin crawled. "And how'd that work out for you?"

Now the Bird Lady spoke rapidly, almost manically, about how the magic had played out. Her wish *had* come true, but not precisely as she'd anticipated. "Magic can be fluky," she cautioned. "Remember that."

"You bet," Ava said.

First of all, the Bird Lady explained, the magic only worked with certain people. As in, the Bird Lady only saw the hopes and dreams of thirteen-year-old girls. Also, sometimes the Bird Lady interpreted things incorrectly. Other times, she looked into someone's eyes and saw nothing.

"What was your second wish, the wish you could make come true yourself?"

The Bird Lady looked ruefully at her hands. "That I *would* admit to what I'd done, but only if someone specifically asked."

Ava snort-laughed. "As in, someone would have to say, 'Hey, did you happen to wish for the ability to look into someone's eyes and see their soul?'"

The Bird Lady smiled and hitched her shoulders. Ave felt sucker punched. She felt embarrassed, and angry for feeling embarrassed, but she tried not to give the Bird Lady the satisfaction of showing it.

"Actually, I bound my wish more tightly to myself than that," the Bird Lady said. "*If* someone specifically asked, I would tell the truth. But I *couldn't* tell the truth *unless* someone asked. Couldn't, not wouldn't. Do you understand the difference?"

"I understand that you made a crazy wish," Ava said.

"I suppose I knew I was crossing a line, in a way," the Bird Lady mused.

In fits and starts, she told Ava what she'd told herself at the time: that yes, she made her first wish knowing that wasn't how the magic was supposed to be used. But she convinced herself that her second wish made it okay. She wouldn't *lie* about it, after all.

"I'm older now, and hopefully wiser," the Bird Lady said. "I accept accountability for my foolishness, but—those were the wishes I made."

"And your third wish?" Ava asked. "The deepest wish of your secret heart?"

"I would prefer not to comment on that," she said in a peculiar tone. Ava thought she saw her chin wobble, but it might have been a trick of the light.

"So what happened?" Ava asked. "You made your impossible wish in order to become popular. Did it work?"

"It did not. Even with my new ability . . ." She trickled off. "I suppose I was still too awkward. I blurted things out. I made everyone uncomfortable, more so than I had before. Oh, pet, those were sad times."

The Bird Lady reached over and patted Ava's hand. Her skin was almost feathery. "My friends, or rather my *peers*, grew up, moved on, and settled into normal lives, while I fell more and more to the wayside. I took on an identity entirely without meaning to." She snorted. "'The town's resident eccentric.' Have you ever?"

Ava smiled uneasily.

"So, I decided to try a new tactic. Maybe if I helped other girls make their dreams come true, then girls would need me, admire me, *like* me."

The Bird Lady told Ava about a girl named Gemma who loved to sing. The Bird Lady's gift allowed her to see Gemma's dreams: She longed to be a famous singer when she grew up. So, on her Wishing Day, Gemma planned to wish that at the upcoming audition for the school musical, she would sing as well as Judy Garland.

"Do you know who Judy Garland is?" the Bird Lady asked Ava. "She was Dorothy in *The Wizard of Oz*."

"My sisters and I watch that movie every Thanksgiving," Ava said.

"Well, I thought Gemma was aiming too low—"

"Too low? Judy Garland is amazing!"

"And so I convinced her to wish, at her audition, to have the voice of an angel."

The Bird Lady cut Ava a glance.

Ava opened her mouth, then shut it. *Maybe* an angel would have a better voice than Judy Garland.

"How did her audition go?"

"Gemma sang with the voice of an angel," the Bird Lady said, throwing her hands out as if to say, *What else?* "Unfortunately, as it turned out, humans can't *hear* angels, so Gemma's performance was a bit of a . . . let's just say misfire. There she was, singing her heart out . . ."

"And people heard nothing?" Ava said. She imagined a girl her age, singing and gesturing, her eyes shining. She imagined the other kids, whispering and giggling. The director of the musical, wearing an expression of pure confusion. "That poor girl!"

"There was the loveliest smell of lilacs, though,"

the Bird Lady said. "I just love lilacs, don't you?"

The Bird Lady told Ava another story, a story about a girl named Addie, who loved flowers. Her plants always died, however, so she was going to wish to be a good gardener. Instead, the Bird Lady urged her to wish for a green thumb.

"Let me guess," Ava said wryly.

"Yes, she got a green thumb. Literally, a green thumb." The Bird Lady tipped her head at Ava. "She got the gift of gardening, too, though."

There were other incidents like this—the Bird Lady didn't share all the details—and she told Ava that at long last, she had started thinking that she needed to scale down her help.

Ava suspected that the Bird Lady needed to stop offering "help" at all, but she kept her mouth shut.

"And that's where Klara comes in," the Bird Lady said. "Your mother, that is."

"Yes. My mother." Ava's insides tightened.

"Klara's plan was to wish to be beautiful," the Bird Lady said.

"*Beautiful?*" Ava said, surprised. Her mother *was* beautiful. Was it because of her wish? "But you said earlier . . . I thought she wanted to be special!"

"And she equated 'beautiful' with 'special,'" the

Bird Lady said. "Falsely, I might add. At any rate, when I looked into Klara's soul, I saw that what she really wanted was to impress a certain boy."

Ava squeezed her hands into fists. *Papa.*

"Beauty is fleeting, however—not to mention that Klara was a lovely girl already. So, I went to her on her Wishing Day. I went to her at twelve a.m., the moment her Wishing Day began. I threw pebbles on her window. She pushed it open. We talked, and I . . . I made a teeny-tiny suggestion, a suggestion that wouldn't turn Klara green or leave her unable to utter a sound. Truly, just a simple little suggestion."

Ava's guts clenched and released. For a moment, she feared she was going to throw up. "*You* told my mom to wish she'd won that contest thing instead of Emily?"

The Bird Lady sighed. "I did."

"And you told her to make her wishes early instead of waiting for sunrise? Instead of waiting for Emily?!"

"I did, and I'm very sorry. I wish I hadn't, and obviously I'll—"

"Wait," Ava said. "That means that *you* did this! The magic wasn't punishing my mom. The magic was punishing *you*!"

"There's no need to blow things out of proportion. Things are going to work out in the end," the Bird

Lady wheedled. "After all, you're here!"

"But my mother! And *Emily*!"

"By the time we set things straight, it'll be as if none of it ever happened." The Bird Lady pleaded with Ava with her eyes. "I helped Natasha and Darya, didn't I? I got us this far."

Ava buzzed with angry adrenaline, but anger wouldn't get her anywhere. Anyway, what the Bird Lady was suggesting, or almost-maybe-possibly suggesting, might be in line with what Ava already planned to do.

"I have to go back to the past and make sure you stay out of my mom's business," Ava stated.

"I think you do, yes."

"Make sure you stay out of *everybody's* business." Her breath caught. "Except—crud. You're meddling in *my* business right now!"

"Meddling . . . or clarifying?" asked the Bird Lady. She sounded tired. She sounded, for the first time, like the old lady she was. "I've thought about this for over twenty years, pet. And I've stayed out of other girls' business in the meantime."

Ava thought hard. She turned everything she knew around and around in her head. *She* had come up with this idea, not the Bird Lady. Knowing what the Bird

Lady told her would help her, almost assuredly.

"And someone else will help you as well," the Bird Lady said.

Ava stiffened. "I thought you said you no longer . . . Are you . . . are you looking into my soul?"

"No, pet. The soul of the world, perhaps. The soul of my mistakes? But not your soul, no."

Ava was sucked into a memory—only it wasn't a memory, because it was of something that hadn't happened yet. She saw herself standing at the lake at City Park. She saw another girl standing beside her. She gasped.

"*Tally?*" she said to the Bird Lady.

"She's another piece of the puzzle, isn't she?"

"She is," Ava said. She took a deep in-breath. "Are you saying that Tally's going to help me?"

"I think so, if you ask her. I hope so."

An idea flared to life in Ava's brain, a brilliant idea. "You have to tell me a secret," she instructed the Bird Lady. "Something you've never told *any*one before."

"What in the world for?"

"So that you'll take me seriously," Ava explained. "When I go to you in the past. When I tell you to stop messing around with other girls' wishes."

The Bird Lady nodded, impressed. She thought for

a moment, then told Ava again about how her mother had died soon after she turned thirteen.

"After your birthday, but before your Wishing Day," Ava said.

The Bird Lady gazed at her hands, which were very wrinkled. "Before she died, she took my hands—these hands—and pulled me close. She told me she loved me, and that there was no such thing as 'normal.'" Her voice broke. "She told me that 'normal' was overrated, anyway."

The Bird Lady took Ava's hands. "The very last thing she said to me . . ."

"Yes?"

The Bird Lady pulled Ava toward her. She whispered into Ava's ear.

"Oh!" Ava said, tears springing to her eyes. "That's so—"

"*Shhh,*" the Bird Lady said. "Shhh, now."

She shooed Ava toward the wisteria that hid the hollow of the tree from the rest of the world. "Go on. Be brave. *Be yourself.* And remember that you're doing this not just for your mother, but for Tally's mother as well. Daughters need their mothers, and mothers need their daughters."

"What about you? Will you be . . . ?"

"I'll be fine," the Bird Lady said. For a moment,

she looked pensive. Then she found a smile and lifted her hand in farewell.

Ava pushed herself up and ducked out from within the hollow. Glass soda bottles clinked in her wake, and the smell of leaves and rain and earth greeted her as she straightened to her full height.

Behind her, purple wisteria vines swayed.

Purple, though they were named for the color blue.

I wish Klara Kosrov would notice me.

—NATHANIEL BLOK, AGE FOURTEEN

CHAPTER TWELVE

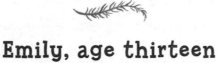

Emily, age thirteen

When Emily reached the lake with her art supplies, including the new pencils Nate had given her for her birthday, she spotted Klara Kosrov curled on one of the bench swings situated around the park. Klara, who shared her birthday. Klara, whose sister Emily had seen roller-skating.

Klara was reading a book. She was barefoot, and her long hair gleamed in the sun.

Emily paused. Should she go to Klara? Wish her happy birthday? She grew shy, and instead sat on the grass near the water. She sketched for a bit. She was happy. A shadow fell over her, and when she looked up and saw Klara standing in front of her, she grew even happier.

"Emily, hi," Klara said. She wore cutoffs and a white camisole. A pale pink bra strap curved across her upper arm. She hooked it with her index finger and pulled it back into place. "Can I join you?"

"Sure," Emily said.

Klara dropped to the grass, leaning back on her palms and offering herself to the sun. "Happy birthday," she said with a grin.

"And to you as well," Emily replied. She grinned, too.

Ripples on the lake glittered. Starlings called out from whispering leaves. Emily knew it was crazy, but she felt the oddest conviction that somehow, she and Klara were occupying a sliver of time untethered from the bonds of seconds and minutes and hours. Or maybe . . . was *all* of time untethered by seconds, minutes, and hours?

Maybe humans chose to count out time on their watches and clocks, and so time obliged, arranging itself into past, present, and future.

But what if, in reality, time was time was time?

She caught Klara looking at her funny and blushed. "I get spacey sometimes," she said. "Sorry."

"No worries," said Klara. "It's part of your charm."

Emily blushed harder.

"I'm kidding!" Klara said. "I mean, I'm not, but it's not a *bad* thing. It's cute."

"Great. I'm charmingly spacey." Emily nodded, determined to let it go at that and not dig herself any deeper. She asked Klara what book she'd been reading—*The Hitchhiker's Guide to the Galaxy*, one of Emily's favorites—and they talked about how cool the idea of alternate realities was.

They moved on to other subjects, and gradually Emily relaxed. Then Klara pulled out a bottle of nail polish and asked if Emily would paint her nails, which made Emily nervous all over again.

"Are you serious?" Emily asked.

"Since you're so good at art," Klara said. "Please?"

"Being good at art means being good at painting nails?"

"I'm not suggesting you grow up to be a manicurist. Just . . ." Klara giggled. "When I paint my own nails, I do a crappy job. Anyone could do a better job than I could."

"Oh. I feel so much better," said Emily. She laughed at Klara's stricken expression and untwisted the lid of the polish. "Kidding. Yes, I'll paint your nails. I might do a crappier job than you, though. I've never done this before."

As Emily brushed pale pink polish onto Klara's fingernails, Klara offered random commentary about various dramas going on at school. Every so often, Emily said "hmm." She'd learned it was best if she stayed out of stuff like that.

Emily coated Klara's left pinky nail with polish, and that was that. All ten fingernails done.

"Nice," Klara said, splaying her fingers.

Using the knuckle of her thumb, Klara tucked a strand of hair behind her ear. She fanned her fingers through the air and returned to talking about school.

"Another thing that drives me crazy," she said. "Have you heard girls say things like, 'I don't have any female friends. I'm only friends with guys'? And they say it like they're bragging?"

Emily had overheard plenty of girls going on and on about how awful girls were, when they, themselves, *were* girls. She nodded.

"I do not want to be one of those girls," said Klara adamantly. *"Ever."*

"Me neither," said Emily. A hum in her mind clued her in that Klara wasn't making random conversation. Klara was leading up to something.

"Klara, are you okay?" she asked.

Immediately, she scolded herself. *No.* She was *not* to follow through on the feelings she got, the vibrations or thoughts or messages or whatever. She'd made a pledge to leave people's business to themselves way back in elementary school. She'd done a pretty good job, with occasional slips.

Mainly, the slips had been minor and could be glossed over. Only two instances stood out as reminders that she needed to stay vigilant. Not just for the sake of others, but for her sake, too.

Blurting out loud to a woman on the street that maybe she should quit smoking had made the woman's day (and possibly the rest of her life) awfully complicated, for example.

"What?" the woman had said, affronted. "As if I asked for your permission, little miss."

"It's just . . . the baby," Emily'd said. And then she'd realized that the woman didn't know about the baby. That the woman's husband didn't know about the baby, either.

"Pregnant? You're pregnant, Monica?" he'd said, going pale. "But . . . I've been overseas for eleven months."

Emily wondered what had happened with that

family. Did they stay a family? Did Monica have the baby? Did Monica stop smoking?

And John Blasingame, whose father beat him. He'd left Willow Hill in the sixth grade, slamming everything from his desk into a heavy-duty garbage bag without making eye contact with anyone.

"We're sorry to see you go, John," their teacher had said.

He'd grunted. Emily had seen the bruises on his arms, despite his long-sleeved shirts. He'd kept his head ducked, but thoughts and images from him came at her hard and fast.

A tall woman with a clipboard standing in a dismal living room. A beat-up sofa, a tattooed man with belligerent eyes.

Child protection services. The best interest of your son.

Get out of my house, or I'll shoot you for trespassing.

Emily *hadn't* intervened, not that time. She hadn't messed up by saying something she shouldn't have. The memory of John's last day in Willow Hill was painful for a different reason. What if she *had* spoken up, back in third grade? Nagged John until he'd gone to the teacher, or what if she had gone to the teacher

158

herself? Might things have ended up differently?

Still, the rule Emily tried to follow was to stay out of people's minds as best she could. If people chose to share things with her, fine. Otherwise, her policy was to plug her ears and shut her eyes and go *la la la*.

"Never mind," Emily said to Klara, trying to take back her prying question. "None of my business."

"It's no big deal," Klara said. She looked at Emily speculatively. "But how'd you know something was wrong?"

"Uh . . . I . . ."

Klara moved on without her. She made a wry expression, placing her hands on her thighs and taking care with her nails. "Only, it would be nice to just cut through all that crap. The drama, the posturing, all of it."

"Girl drama, you mean?"

Klara laughed. "Girl drama. Yeah." She hesitated, and Emily knew, once again, that she was working up to something. Emily kept her face neutral.

"I could be mistaken," Klara said, "but I have the feeling you're someone who could do that."

"Do what?"

Klara bit her bottom lip. "Just . . . not be shallow all the time."

"I hope I'm not shallow. I don't want to be."

"That's the thing! I don't think you are!" Klara said fervently. "Like in fifth grade? With that Holly girl?"

Emily wrinkled her nose. Holly, who wore loads of eyeliner and her ironic plaid skirts. Who told Emily that her parents' divorce *was* Emily's fault, regardless of what her parents might or might not have claimed.

"She was a jerk, but you were nice to her," Klara said.

"You remember that?"

Klara shrugged.

"Holly wasn't the greatest," Emily agreed. "But underneath, she seemed sad. People act mean for all sorts of reasons."

"See?" Klara said. "A shallow person wouldn't have said that. A shallow person would have said, 'Holly was a turd. I hope she gets stomped on in a tragic camel stampede.'"

Emily gave her a look.

"Omigosh. Now you're worried about Holly and camels, aren't you?"

"I'm not!" Emily said.

"Protest if you must, but I read you like a book. You, Emily Blok, are genuinely concerned about Holly's risk of camel-trampling, which makes it official:

You are a good person."

Emily felt warm with pleasure. "I'm . . . just me. But thanks." She paused. "I don't want you *or* Holly to get trampled by a camel. For the record."

"For the record, Holly's on her own when the stampeding starts. I'll pull you to freedom, though."

"Thank you."

Klara leaned forward, laughing and hiding her head with her hands. When she pulled her hands away, her fingernails remained as flawless as ten perfect seashells.

"Do you ever wonder why we are who we are?" she asked. "Like, why I'm me and you're you. Why we exist at this exact moment in time?"

Emily felt a tingling sensation all over her body, like the fluttering of tiny honeybee wings. She thought of fireflies and stars and how bright the moon glowed on clear, cold nights. She held Klara's gaze and thought of magic. Klara's eyes widened, telling Emily that she felt it, too.

Energy hummed between them, weaving their souls together, and Emily didn't stick her fingers in her ears and go *la la la*.

Friends, thought Emily. The word felt exotic. *Klara and I are going to be friends.*

Her prediction was slightly off, as it turned out. She and Klara weren't *going* to be friends. They already were. It happened in a heartbeat,

just

like

that.

CHAPTER THIRTEEN

Ava

On the third day of the third month of Ava's thirteenth year, Ava awoke to the smell of bacon. Bacon and pancakes to celebrate Ava's Wishing Day, along with syrup *and* mini-marshmallows, which Aunt Vera strongly disapproved of.

"Such a sweet tooth," she tutted, passing the bowl of tiny marshmallows to Ava. "Where did you get that from? Certainly not from me."

Aunt Elena joined them for breakfast, which was lovely, but which highlighted the fact that Mama stayed away.

At least Angela stayed away, too, Ava thought. She

told herself that Papa understood that Wishing Days were for members of the family, and she chose to find hope in the fact that he honored that. She told herself that he must still long for Mama. Angela couldn't replace her. No one could.

The meal was a mishmash of happy banter and sticky syrup fingers. Everyone fussed over Ava, and when Aunt Vera refused to let the girls help clean up the dishes, they happily obliged. Natasha led them to the rope swing Papa had made, which had a wooden plank to sit on. Mama used to love the swing. She still would, if she were here.

And she will be, Ava told herself firmly.

Natasha and Darya allowed Ava to sit on the swing since this was her special day. Natasha pushed her from behind, and Darya, standing in front of Ava, return-pushed her in the opposite direction, pressing her hands to Ava's bare feet and shoving. She felt like their plaything as they passed her back and forth. As they outlined their plan for how and when Ava would carry out the ritual of her Wishing Day, she felt even more so.

"We'll climb to the top of Willow Hill as soon as the moon comes out," said Natasha.

"All three of us," said Darya. "I don't think we

need the aunts. Do you, Natasha?"

"I don't think we should bother Mama, either," said Natasha, and the way she phrased it stung. A mother should *want* to be there for her daughter's Wishing Day. It shouldn't be "a bother." But if Natasha and Darya were going along with the group lie, who was Ava to break rank?

"Once we're at the top of the hill, we'll let you go to the willow tree by yourself," Natasha went on. "But we'll stay close. Ten feet away."

"And you know what to do, right?" asked Darya. "Touch the bark and make your wishes?"

"Sounds good," Ava said.

It did, in theory. Just, Ava had her own plan already in place. For hers to work, she had to agree with her sisters. She had to go along with their assumption that she'd carry out her Wishing Day the way they'd carried out theirs, at the ancient willow at the top of Willow Hill. That she'd touch the bark, close her eyes . . . do everything just like they'd done it, as if that were the law.

It wasn't. Girls could make their Wishing Day wishes however they wanted. For Ava's sisters, as well as Mama, Aunt Vera, and Aunt Elena, as well as their mother before them and so on, making their wishes at the willow tree was a time-honored tradition. But sometimes traditions had to be broken, because sometimes cycles needed to broken.

Ava felt guilty for misleading Natasha and Darya, but only slightly. They were pushing her around, literally—and why?

Because they saw her as a baby.

She considered what Aunt Elena had said, about how Natasha, Darya, and Ava were a unit, and that one day Ava might miss being treated like the baby. Not today.

"Will you two please stop pushing me?" she said. "If I don't quit swinging, I'm going to faint."

When they didn't comply, she said, "Or throw up. If you don't stop pushing me, I'll throw up. I mean it."

Natasha grabbed the ropes and stilled the swing, and Ava hopped off. The world swayed.

"You are the best sisters in the world," she said as she headed across the yard. "Thanks for everything!"

"Where are you going?" Darya called, exasperated.

"For a walk, just to think about things. I'll be back!"

"Think about *what*?" asked Darya. "What you're going to wish for?"

"Uh-huh," Ava replied without turning around.

"That's good," Natasha said, always the oldest sister. "Just remember: You can't wish for anything foolish or dangerous or whatever. You *can't* go against me on this, Ava. I love you too much to risk letting you get hurt."

"Uh-huh!" Ava repeated.

"Believe it or not, I do too," Darya said. "Would you turn around?"

Ava stopped, took a breath, and turned around. She pasted on a compliant-little-sister look of confusion. "Yeah?"

"We *all* love you, me and Darya, Mama and Papa, Aunt Vera and Aunt Elena," said Natasha. "So, do you promise to make your wishes carefully?"

"Natasha, we've talked about this," Ava said. "Don't you trust me?"

For a microsecond, Natasha regarded her suspiciously. Then she smiled and shook her head, rolling her eyes at herself for thinking that little Ava would defy her older, wiser sisters.

CHAPTER FOURTEEN

Emily, age thirteen

Emily fell hard and fast into the friendship Klara offered. Maybe it was because Emily had never had a best friend before. Maybe it was because Klara was so comfortable expressing her affection for Emily that Emily felt bold enough to do the same. There was no jealousy or jockeying for position, not that Emily could detect. For a little while, Emily stayed on the alert, wondering if all this was too good to be true. Could becoming friends with someone happen so naturally?

As their friendship deepened, Emily realized she didn't need to label whatever magical alchemy bound them together. Why ask why an orange was called an orange and not a lemon? Why ask why an orange *was* an orange, when the answer smiled coyly from its tangy pulp?

An orange was an orange was an orange.

Emily and Klara were Emily and Klara; Klara and Emily were Klara and Emily.

Klara went home from school with Emily one afternoon during the first week of April, and Emily introduced her to Nate. They already knew who the other was, so it wasn't a big deal. Klara's reaction, however, came to Emily as a shock.

Klara *liked* Nate, like in a crush sort of way . . . and Nate liked Klara. Their crush-feelings were too strong for Emily to block. Emily couldn't decide whether to be amused or horrified.

"The Academic Olympiad?" Nate said after Klara stammered something about how she and Emily were working on a school project due in May. "Yeah, I did that in seventh grade. It was a lot of work."

"Was it?" Klara asked. She giggled, her voice too high. "I mean, I know I won't win, but I'll do my best. Unless I get distracted. Sometimes I get distracted." She blushed. "Please pretend I'm making actual sense."

"When I entered, I submitted a plan for how to build a lute," Nate said. "It had nothing to do with any of the questions, but it was what I wanted to spend my time on." His blush matched hers. "Does that count as distracted?"

Klara giggled again, and Emily cocked her head, fascinated. Would a boy have an effect like this on her someday? Would *she* affect a boy like this someday? It seemed far-fetched, but here it was happening right in front of her eyes. Not to herself, but to her best friend. To her best friend *and* her brother!

She didn't mind, she discovered after poking and prodding her insides. For one thing, they weren't ready for any sort of romance. Klara was a seventh grader. Nate was two grades older.

Also, Emily trusted Klara's feelings for her as well as her brother's feelings for her. Emily wasn't a third wheel. Instead, there were two overlapping sets of wheels: Emily and Klara, as best friends, and Emily and Nate, as sister and brother.

The biggest reason she didn't mind was because . . .

She blushed. But *if* one day Klara and Nate did date, did fall in love, did, ah, get married . . .

If that happened, what an abundance of love. She and Klara would be sisters, or sisters-in-law. She grinned, and Klara shot her an embarrassed grin in return.

After settling down with snacks in Emily's room, Emily asked Klara flat out if she liked Nate. She already knew the answer, but if she asked, and Klara answered, then there'd be less of a chance of Emily slipping up and referring to Klara's crush by accident.

Klara leaned against the end of Emily's bed and pursed her lips. They were sitting on the carpet so that they wouldn't get Dorito dust on Emily's comforter. Klara's hands rested on her lap, forming a bird's nest for her chips.

"I do," Klara said. "But I'm not allowed to go out with boys until high school, so it's not, like . . . you know." She swiveled her head to look at Emily. "Do you mind?"

"It's weird, but nah, I'm okay with it," Emily said.

There was a knock on the door, and Emily's mom entered before getting permission.

"Well, *hello*!" she said in an overly bright voice.

"Hi, Mom," said Emily.

"Hi, Mrs. Blok," said Klara.

Emily's mom smiled at Emily and Klara expectantly. Emily shifted uncomfortably. What did her mother want?

Her mother's smile grew strained. She gave Emily a

meaningful look, and Emily pushed tentatively at her mother's thoughts.

Oh. Der.

"Mom, this is Klara," she said. "Klara, this is my mom."

"What a *pleasure* to meet you, Klara," said Emily's mom.

"It's nice to meet you, too," Klara said politely.

"I'm thrilled you and Emily are friends. I hope you'll teach her how to talk to people without scaring them away!" She trilled a giddy laugh.

Emily wanted to sink through the floor. *"Mom."*

"Klara knows I'm teasing," her mom said, waving away Emily's concern. "Or, I'm *not*"—again, that giddy laugh—"but I only say it out of love. You know that, Klara, don't you?"

"I don't know," Klara said. "Emily is pretty scary."

Emily's mom blinked. Then she said, "Now *you're* teasing *me*, you funny girl." She pulled her features together in an odd way. "People don't really think she's scary, do they?"

Klara shot Emily a look. Emily was too mortified to respond.

"Everyone thinks Emily's great," Klara said with a shrug. "Plus, she's the best artist in the school. Did you know that?"

"Yes, Emily is quite talented," Emily's mom acknowledged. "I suppose artists have the right to be eccentric."

"I guess," Klara mused. "Is she eccentric, though? She's . . . just Emily."

She's just Emily, Emily imagined her dad saying. *For heaven's sake, Rose, let her be herself.*

Longing stabbed Emily's heart. She missed her father terribly.

Emily's mother studied Klara, noting her cute outfit, her cute hairstyle, her cute everything. Emily heard her thoughts loud and clear:

If only Emily . . .

Maybe Klara will rub off on her?

It's a start, at any rate.

"She painted my nails," Klara blurted. She transferred her remaining chips into one palm and held out her fingers for Emily's mom to see. "She's painted them three different times for me. She's really good."

Emily's mother put her hand to her chest and made a small sound, her mouth a perfect O. Eyes shining, she crossed the room, leaned over, and gave Klara a hug.

"Mom!" Emily said.

"I adored having mani-pedi parties with my friends when I was your age!" Emily's mother gushed. "I am just . . . I'm so . . ." She made that small sound once more, an almost animal sound of gratitude. "You have fun, girls. And Klara, you are *always* welcome here, okay, hon?"

Beaming, she backed out of the room and pulled the door shut behind her.

Klara looked at Emily.

Emily looked at Klara.

Klara giggled. Her giggling grew, and Emily cast aside her horror and joined in. Their laughter was mutinous and exhilarating: Emily and Klara versus her mom. Emily's chest expanded. The "and Klara" part made all the difference.

"Your mom," Klara managed when they'd passed the laughing-est part of their fit.

"I warned you," Emily said.

"She *hugged* me for introducing you to the feminine art of nail polish," Klara said. "Is she always like that?"

Emily blew air out of puffed cheeks. "I'm not exactly the daughter she wants me to be."

"That's ridiculous. You're a great daughter!"

"I know she loves me. Just, she thinks I'm weird."

"So? What's wrong with weird?"

"I remind her of her mother."

174

"Does she not like her mother?"

"It's fine. Don't worry."

Emily felt Klara's gaze rake across her. *Don't hug me*, Emily begged, knowing that such an act of kindness would undo her. *Don't do it, Klara.*

"Come here," Klara said, sliding her arm around Emily's shoulder and pulling her close.

Emily fought back tears.

"Shhh," Klara murmured. "You're okay."

Emily let the words wash over her, and she didn't come undone after all.

*I wish I could go to Willow Hill again. I wish
I could remember where Willow Hill is!*

—EMILY BLOK, AGE UNKNOWN

CHAPTER FIFTEEN

Ava

As Ava escaped from her sisters, it occurred to her that there *was* a benefit of being labeled the baby of the family: No one was scared of babies. No one looked at babies suspiciously, wondering if they might be up to no good. If the baby wasn't crying, then great. The baby was fine and no need to worry.

Stealth mode. Ava could work with that.

It took her fifteen minutes to walk to Tally's house. When she reached the cluttered yard of Tally's foster parents, she slowed from a purposeful stride to a purposeful . . . stall.

No, she told herself, straightening her spine. *No chickening out!*

She stepped over a miniature plastic grocery cart that lay on its side and punched the doorbell.

"Hi!" said the woman who answered the door. "Can I help you?" She had short, grayish blond hair, cut so that the front hung longer than the back. She was small and plain, but her smile was warm.

"Hi," Ava said. "I'm—"

"One of the Blok girls! Everyone knows the Blok girls!"

Ava braced herself.

"Let's see, you're the youngest, aren't you?" Tally's foster mom said. "Come on in. I'll call Tally." She opened the door wider, revealing a hoarder's heaven of magazines, overflowing boxes, and random appliances. A microwave sat on an old-fashioned square TV.

"Tally!"

There was a patter of footsteps, and Tally appeared in the hall. Scowling, she brushed past her foster mom and grabbed Ava's upper arm. "Bye, Deanne," she said, pulling Ava with her.

"Bye, Mrs.—" Ava broke off. She didn't know Tally's foster mother's last name. "Tally," she said, stumbling as she tried to keep up. "Tally, what's wrong? Will you please slow down?"

Tally released Ava's arm, but maintained her speed

walker's pace. "Why are you here? Where's Darya?"

"I'm not attached to Darya by the hip, thank you very much."

"*At* the hip."

"Huh?"

"The expression is *at* the hip."

Ava considered. Tally might be right, since being attached at the hip would describe two people with their arms around each other, for example. Being attached *by* the hip would be like saying attached *by* a string, which would imply, like, dangling. Ava did not "dangle" from Darya or Natasha.

"Whatever," Ava said.

It was May. It wasn't yet hot, but it was warm enough to make Ava's hair feel heavy against her neck. She pulled a ribbon elastic off her wrist and gathered her hair into a bunch. Deftly, she swooped her hair through and twisted the elastic. She repeated the process until she was left with a nice, tight ponytail.

Tally side-eyed her.

"What?"

"You reminded me of someone for a second."

"Who?"

Tally shook her head. "Listen, I don't like people coming to Deanne and Troy's house."

"Deanne and Troy are . . . ?"

"My foster parents."

"Why? Do you not like them?"

"I like them fine. I just don't like people showing up unannounced."

"Got it. Sorry."

Tally took several brisk strides, then exhaled. She slowed down, though not by much.

"What's going on?" Tally asked. "What do you need me for? Does it have to do with Darya?"

"It kind of does. But . . ." She steered the two of them to the left instead of continuing straight ahead. She checked over her shoulder. Tally followed, but looked put out.

"I thought we could go to the lake," Ava said.

"Why?"

Because, Ava thought. *Because of life, the universe, and everything, and because that's where I need you to help me.*

"Will you tell me about your mom?" Ava asked.

"My *mom*? Why?"

Because of life, the universe . . .

"Because today's my Wishing Day."

Tally cut her a look. "Whoop-de-do," she said. She had moved to Willow Hill when she was thirteen and

182

a half. She hadn't been granted a Wishing Day.

"I want to make my wishes carefully," Ava said. "I *have* to. For one thing, it's my only chance. Also, you may not believe in any of this, but my wishes have a good chance of coming true. I know that sounds dumb, but it's something that runs in my family. The magic, I mean."

Ugh. She was babbling. She lifted her chin and said, "In my family, the magic tends to work. My ancestors are the ones who brought it here."

"If you say so," said Tally.

"It's not that I say so. The magic says so." She shrugged. "Magic is weird."

"'Magic is *weird*'?" Tally said. They reached the footpath that cut through to City Park, where the lake was. "Ava, your whole family is weird."

"I know!" Ava said. "That's why I wanted to talk to you. That's why I need you to come with me to the lake."

"Ava—"

"That's why I asked about your mom," Ava said hurriedly, her heart rate bumping up. "I've seen the picture you drew of her."

Tally's eyes darkened. She stopped walking. "What picture?"

"I think you know, but . . . here." From the pocket of her cutoffs, Ava pulled out a drawing Tally had torn up and thrown away months ago. Darya, without Tally's knowledge, had retrieved it and taped it back together. Ava, without *Darya's* knowledge, had later appropriated the drawing for reasons of her own.

She passed the folded piece of paper to Tally, who accepted it reluctantly. When she unfolded it, the color drained from her face.

"Where did you get this?"

"It *is* your mom, right?" Ava asked. "You drew it based on a photo of her. I heard Darya say so."

Tally started walking. Ava stayed by her side, matching Tally's pace as they neared the lake. In the distance, Ava could spot the rustic bench swings she'd always adored.

"My mom recognized her from your drawing," Ava said. "*My* mom recognized *your* mom, whose name is Emily. Her name was written on the back of the photo."

"So?"

"*So*, my mom's best friend was named Emily, as you know."

"Only she never actually existed, according to Darya."

"And my dad had—or hopefully *has*—a little sister." Ava swallowed. "Her name is Emily, too."

Tally tightened her jaw.

"And your mom, whose name, you know, is Emily, doesn't remember her past," Ava said.

"She remembers her past," Tally said. "Just not well. Not all of it."

"What *does* she remember?"

Tally didn't want to talk about it, Ava could tell. "She lived with her dad's grandmother for a while. Then I guess she got kicked out or something. Sometimes she lived on the streets. Sometimes in foster homes. What does this have to do with you?"

Ava felt the blue, blue sky pressing down on her. Maybe Tally's mom remembered her past; maybe she didn't. That didn't matter. What mattered was that Tally's heart hurt. Tally was lonely and full of pain.

The words Ava needed were *right there*, if only she could grab them.

She jogged forward and grabbed Tally's forearm. "Tally, wait up."

Tally shook Ava off. *"What?!"*

"You said my family's weird," Ava said. "I said you're right."

"Fantastic," said Tally. "And I care because . . . ?"

"Because I think you're part of my weird family. I think your mom is my dad's little sister." She took a breath. "Tally, we're cousins."

CHAPTER SIXTEEN

Emily, age thirteen

"You're going to win, you know," said Klara.

"Oh, please," said Emily. It was the beginning of May, and she and Klara were lying on their backs at City Park. They'd turned in their Academic Olympiad projects that afternoon, and Emily felt light and airy. She thought of starfish and snow angels. She imagined rising into the sky.

"*You* oh, please," Klara countered. "You're, like, the smartest girl in our grade."

"First of all, ha. Anyway, I didn't even answer the final question, the one about freedom or whatever."

"Freedom of expression: Is it worth fighting for?"

Klara said in a stuffy, scholarly voice. "What does it mean to be 'free'? Illustrate using examples from the past, present, or future."

Emily groaned.

"You wrote *some*thing," Klara said.

"I wrote nothing."

"You left the page blank? For real?"

"I didn't leave it *blank*. I drew a picture."

"Shut up," Klara said. "Are you serious?"

Emily let the sun warm her skin. "I am as serious as a . . . oh, I can't even think what I'm as serious as."

Klara laughed. "No. Way. Emily, you're brilliant without even meaning to be."

"Um, not following."

"Instead of writing some boring essay about how important freedom of expression is, blah blah blah, *you* freely expressed yourself, and you did so by actually illustrating . . . whatever you illustrated."

"Don't be ridiculous."

"I'm not."

"It's just a dumb contest," Emily said. "Honestly, I don't care about winning."

"Winning would be fun, though," Klara said.

"I guess. But if it came down to me winning or you, I'd pick you."

Klara said, "*Awwww*. Brilliant and selfless. Practically perfect in every way."

Emily rolled onto her side and propped her head on her palm, debating whether to bring up something that was gently but insistently tugging at her. With Klara, as with Nate and her mom, Emily had decided early on not to intentionally invade her thoughts.

Sometimes things slipped through anyway, and beneath Klara's breezy manner, Emily sensed a thrum of worry.

And you are her friend, Emily told herself. *Friends look after each other.*

She cleared her throat. "Hey, Klara, I feel like something's on your mind."

Klara stared at the clouds.

"Are you okay?" Emily pressed.

Klara rolled onto her side to face Emily, matching her head-on-palm position. "How do you do that?"

"Do what?"

"Know when something's wrong. If I'm worried or upset or whatever, you always know."

Emily shrugged and reminded herself to hold back as best she could. Hold back, but also be there for Klara—a tricky mix. "You do the same for me."

"I try."

"You do," Emily insisted. She hesitated. "So, something *is* wrong?"

"Not wrong, really. But do you know that old lady, the crazy lady everyone calls the Bird Lady?"

"I know of her." The Bird Lady was homeless, Emily knew that. In fact, the Bird Lady was possibly the only homeless person in all of Willow Hill. "My mom tells me to stay away from her."

"Why?"

"Because she's my mom. Because the Bird Lady . . . well, she doesn't exactly wear stockings and pumps and 'proper' grown-up lady clothes, does she?"

Klara laughed. "I suppose not."

"I once saw her wearing a dress made entirely out of candy bar wrappers."

"That's impressive, actually."

"I thought so, too!" Emily swiped a strand of hair off her face. "My mom says she should be institutionalized."

"That's harsh. Do you?"

"I think she's her own person, and I'm okay with that. I also think—*know*—that my mom is as far from okay with that as possible. In my mother's perfect world, everyone would act appropriately, think appropriately, and absolutely dress appropriately, always.

190

And my mother would be the one who got to decide what was appropriate or not."

Emily saw the Bird Lady in her mind, scattering birdseed for the ever-present birds that flocked around her. "If the Bird Lady were really someone to fear, I don't think the birds would trust her."

"Like how dogs have built-in jerk detectors?" said Klara.

"Animals are better judges of character than humans, some people say." Emily furrowed her brow. "But what's going on? Did something happen that involved the Bird Lady?"

"Well, yeah," Klara said. She gave a puzzled smile. "Yesterday I was at the flower garden by the senior center, where the gazebo is. I was reading *Slaughterhouse-Five* and trying to get some sun, so I don't look like such a codfish now that summer's coming." She wiggled her toes, drawing attention to her slim, pale legs.

Emily, with her pale skin, would stay codfish white all the way through August. Codfish white or lobster red.

"Anyway, the Bird Lady just kind of . . . appeared and plopped down beside me, out of the blue," Klara said. "She was wearing a bright-orange jumpsuit, like what someone doing roadwork might wear."

"Ah," Emily said. "Was she doing roadwork?"

"She mentioned my Wishing Day, and how it's coming up soon."

"In two weeks. Mine too."

"Yeah," Klara said, nudging Emily's foot. "But how did the Bird Lady know?" She twisted a strand of hair around her finger. "She said to be careful what I wish for."

"Ooo, because you just might receive it?" Emily said. She made spooky fingers. "Yeah, yeah, yeah."

"Then she took my book—just took it out of my hands—flipped to a certain page, and read a section out loud."

"Of *Slaughterhouse-Five*?" Emily said.

Slaughterhouse-Five was brilliant. Klara and Emily both thought so. But for the Bird Lady to take it out of Klara's hands . . .

Emily was fine with weird. But Emily wouldn't take a book out of a random person's hands.

Klara sat up, dug through her backpack, and lay back down with the battered paperback. She flipped to the middle and handed it to Emily. "She pretended to read straight from the book, but when I went back and checked, she'd . . . paraphrased, more like."

Emily scanned the page. "The bit about time? Is

that what she read—or kind of read?"

Klara nodded. "The part about how time is like a fly trapped in amber. How we see each moment in time as if it's frozen, and that every moment has always occurred and always will occur."

Emily read aloud: "'All time is all time, it does not change or lend itself to explanations—it simply is.'"

"Yeah."

"And she wanted to share that with you?" Emily asked. "Did she say why?"

"She did not."

"Did it have to do with your Wishing Day?"

"Probably, wouldn't you think?"

Emily shifted as a honeybee buzzed lazily past. She followed it with her eyes, thinking that the honeybee *wasn't* trapped in amber, obviously. Emily wished she understood the Kurt Vonnegut quote. It sounded cool. What did it mean, though?

"Did it freak you out?" Emily asked.

"That's the craziest part. It didn't," Klara said. "At least, not when it happened. But the more I think about it . . ." She exhaled. "Who knows? Maybe she's nuts. Maybe she honestly just wanted to remind me not to make my wishes lightly."

"A public service announcement," said Emily.

Klara half laughed. "Sure. Yeah."

Emily looked at Klara, and Klara held her gaze, open and unguarded. There were so many colors in Klara's eyes. Not just brown, but brown flecked with gold, green, and even pinpricks of dusty rose.

"What *are* you going to wish for?" Emily asked. "If you want to talk about it, that is."

"I do, if you do. Unless you think it's illegal or something."

"Wishing Day Jail? That would not be good." Emily hesitated. "But Klara, don't ask me. You're the expert on all this."

"I'm no expert."

"Your family, then. My mom didn't even make her Wishing Day wishes." She considered that for a moment. "I bet *she* thinks it's illegal."

"I think we should make our wishes together," Klara said, animated. She pushed herself into a sitting position. "Like . . . at sunrise, at the ancient willow tree at the top of Willow Hill."

Emily sat up. She envisioned herself and Klara side by side, bathed in the hues of the rising sun. Emily loved sunrises. She was obsessed with catching them in a sketch one day, but their wealth of colors made it a challenge: pink, tangerine, the milky haze of lavender, as well as a yellow-blue color sometimes referred to in art books as the "forbidden color."

Normally, yellow mixed with blue became green: kindergarten finger-painting science at its finest. But during sunrise, the light frequencies of yellow and blue didn't cancel each other out. Rather, they flooded into each other, creating an ethereal color that didn't have a name.

"The top of Willow Hill at sunrise," Emily said. "Okay, let's do a practice run. You first."

"Here, or Willow Hill?"

"Here. Our wishes, that's all."

Klara lifted one eyebrow.

"I'll show you mine if you show me yours," Emily said.

"Naughty girl," Klara teased.

"Thought I was practically perfect."

"Who says you can't be both?"

Emily grinned.

Klara lifted her hair and dropped it over her shoulders. "Well, for my impossible wish—*and no laughing*—I'm thinking . . . maybe . . . of wishing to be beautiful." She said the last bit in a rush, and her cheeks reddened.

Emily's reaction surprised herself. It surprised Klara, too. Emily could sense it.

"You're mad," Klara said.

"What? No, Klara, I'm not—" Emily broke off. "Why would I be *mad*?"

"You disapprove, then. Why?"

Emily wasn't sure. There was nothing wrong with beauty. Just, for Klara to use a wish to change her appearance . . . Klara, who began their friendship with a heartfelt pledge not to be superficial . . .

It seemed very un-Klara-like.

Then Emily saw it, the real motive behind Klara's wish.

Klara wants to be beautiful for Nate, Emily gleaned.

Emily considered telling Klara that Nate already liked her, that he'd keep liking her, and that anyway, he thought she was beautiful already. Only she couldn't, not without explaining her whole . . . gift thing.

"Wish for whatever you want," Emily ended up saying. "I mean, you already are beautiful, but Klara, it's your wish. Whatever *you* want is what *I* want for you." She pretended to be stern. "Yes, ma'am?"

"Yes, ma'am," Klara said, relaxing. "Thank you for not making fun of me."

"I would never!"

"I know, which brings me to—drumroll, please— my second wish, the wish I can make come true myself.

I'm going to wish to stay best friends with you forever."

Emily melted. "Klara!"

"And for the deepest wish of my secret heart?" Klara said. She grew solemn. "I've thought about this a lot. It might not make sense, exactly . . . but what part of this does, right?"

Emily waited.

"The deepest wish of my secret heart is that magic *is* real," Klara said. Her eyes were luminous. "Because if it is, and my wishes come true, my life will be pretty much perfect."

Because of Nate, Emily thought, pierced by a stab of jealousy. She shook herself. *No, because of Nate* and *because of me*, she corrected herself. She reminded herself of another kindergarten lesson: Love was not a cup of sugar, and love didn't run out. There was always enough to go around.

"I don't need much," Klara continued. "I want to grow up and get married and have a family. Maybe have three daughters, just like my mom. Maybe that sounds boring and predictable, but that's what I want. I *want* to be a good mom and a good wife and a good friend . . ."

Klara's voice hitched, and Emily's heart skipped a beat.

"Klara," she said. "Hey. *Hey*. There's nothing wrong with any of that. Do you think I'm going to judge you? I'm not!"

"You might. You could. I wouldn't blame you if you did. I know how you feel about . . ." Her sentence trickled off.

"About what?" asked Emily. "It would be one thing if you told me you wanted to . . . I don't know, be a bank robber or a serial killer or . . ." She groped for better examples, then gave up and said, "But Klara, wanting to get married and have kids and be happy, all of that is completely—"

Oh.

Normal. A normal life was the life Klara dreamed of.

Emily's chest rose and fell. Klara tried to speak, but Emily raised her hand, silencing her.

"I understand now," she said. "But Klara, there's nothing wrong with wanting those things. There really isn't. I want those things, too."

"You do?" asked Klara.

"Friends, family, a happy life?" Emily said. "Sure."

"I was just worried . . . well, that—"

"I'd feel as if you were rejecting me, just like my mom," Emily filled in.

"Or that *you'd* reject *me*, for following the herd or

198

whatever," Klara said.

"No," said Emily. She knew Klara wasn't coming down on her. Still, she felt the sinking sensation of having done something wrong, the dread of being scolded.

"My mom's version of 'normal' is different from yours," Emily said.

"Very," Klara quickly said.

Emily tried to sort through her emotions. Her mother made her feel bad for not conforming to the definition of "normal" that her mother subscribed to. Feeling bad . . . well, it felt *bad*. It did.

Emily knew that her mother's concern sprang from love. What she didn't know was if her mother refused to accept Emily for who she was—in other words, not "normal"—or if her mother was just . . .

Flawed?

That's what it felt like, but surely that wasn't fair.

What if her mom simply didn't possess enough imagination to see Emily for who she truly was?

She'd been silent for an awfully long time, she realized.

Klara sat there, kind of wringing her hands.

"Um, I think it's one thing to reject being normal if being 'normal' means not being who you really are," Emily said carefully. She saw hope in Klara's eyes, which gave her courage. What might it feel like to forgive herself—as well as her mother? Was Emily capable of separating herself from her mom's expectations?

A wet, woolen weight loosened its hold on her.

"But deciding for yourself what makes you happy, and then doing everything you can to make that happen . . . I have a feeling that's the *only way* to be happy," Emily continued. "So, Klara, if what you want is a normal life, normal by *your* standards, that's what you should go for."

"Really?" Klara said.

"Really," Emily insisted.

Klara studied her. Then she gave Emily a funny, squinty smile. "Well . . . all right, then." Klara rearranged her legs so that she was sitting cross-legged. "Now it's your turn. Let's hear your wishes."

Emily drew her thumbnail to her mouth. She pulled it out. "All right. For the deepest wish of my secret heart . . ."

Several long moments ticked by.

"You're stalling," Klara chastised.

"I'm not," Emily protested. "I'm just not sure what words to use."

Klara raised her hand as if they were in school. "I have an idea. How about you use the words that say what your deepest wish is?"

"Thanks, yeah," said Emily.

Klara lowered her hand and smirked.

"I need to figure out how to phrase it before our Wishing Days, but basically, my deepest wish is to be closer to my dad." Saying it out loud prompted a wellspring of tears. She swiped at her eyes. "Sorry."

"Oh, Em, no need to be sorry," Klara said, scooching over and putting her arm around her. "When you say 'closer,' do you mean physically closer or emotionally closer?"

"Both, but physically would be a good start. Like, why can't I go visit him in California? Spend time with him?"

"Because your mom doesn't want you to, which is really, really unfair. You could go to a judge, I bet. Or get your dad to go to a judge!"

"I've thought of that," Emily said. "Just, it's complicated. I don't want to hurt my mom, but I do want my dad to be part of my life." She picked at a loose thread on her cutoffs. "He understands me better. Before he moved, before my parents got divorced, he was the one who stood up for me. He said things like, 'There's no such thing as normal.'"

Klara took Emily's hand.

"Not a one-size-fits-everyone kind of normal, I mean," Emily clarified, not wanting Klara to feel bad again for saying she wanted a normal life.

"An excellent wish," Klara said.

"Thanks." Emily squeezed Klara's hand, then released it.

"And for the wish you can make come true yourself?"

"Same as yours: for us to stay best friends forever."

"*Aw*," Klara said. "We're so cheesy, aren't we?"

Emily smiled. "We are."

"And your impossible wish?"

Emily saw herself as a little girl, sitting on her knees in the backseat of her parents' station wagon and facing backward. Looking out the rear window, the world had seemed enormous.

Her dad had turned on the car, and her mom had said, "Turn around, Emily. Fasten up." As her dad backed the car out of the driveway, she'd taken in the wide blue sky visible through the side window. Then the sky through Nate's window, on the opposite side. The sky was everywhere, and she was the sky. She was the world. She was everything.

A smile had stretched across her face. She'd wanted to put what she knew into words, but her mother had clicked on the radio, and the song sent the words swirling away. Sent the moment swirling away, forgotten until this moment of basking in the sun with Klara.

"The truth?" Emily said. "To be older. To be past all of this."

"Past all of what? The stuff with your mom and dad?"

"It's kind of the same as what you want, actually: a happy life. Because when I'm older—"

"How much older?"

"Eighteen?" Emily said, trying it out. "Done with high school?" She looked inside herself. "Old enough to move out of my mom's house and be *me*. To be *my* kind of normal, without my mom making me feel like a constant failure."

"But Emily!"

"What?"

"You can't just skip over"—Klara counted on her fingers—"*five years* of your life. Five years?!"

"Why not?"

"For one, wouldn't you miss me?"

"Well . . . I don't think so."

Klara made a sound of wounded indignation.

"No, wait! Only because I wouldn't *be here* to miss you. In theory, yes, of course I'd miss you. But if the wish worked, I'd jump straight to eighteen, and there you'd be."

"Well, *I'd* miss *you*," Klara argued.

"No, because it's not like I would disappear or anything. I'd still *live* those years. I just wouldn't . . . experience it? This me"—she tapped her chest—"would flash forward to high school graduation, that's all."

"How many yous are there?" Klara asked. "And what if . . ." She pursed her lips. "All right, what if I die between now and graduation? Wouldn't you want to be there for that?"

"For your death?"

Klara looked at her. "You know what I mean."

Emily envisioned a room in a funhouse, filled with mirrors. Emily after Emily after Emily, girl after girl after girl. Choice after choice after choice. And now Klara—the most alive person she knew—dying?

The conversation, already absurd, had only grown more so. She giggled.

"Omigosh," Klara huffed. "I tell you I could *die*, and you laugh."

"Klara, you're not going to die."

"I might. A shark could eat me."

"A land shark? A lake shark?"

Klara pulled a face. "Fine. A tree could fall on my head."

"Ah. But if a tree falls on your head, and no one is there to hear it . . ."

Klara shoved her. Emily toppled, but caught herself.

"Please don't die, Klara," she said. "There's only one of you. You need to stay safe."

"The same goes for you," said Klara. "And don't go away, either." She shoved Emily harder, and this time Emily stayed where she landed, sprawled on the grass. She stretched out her arms, forming a T with her body. She gazed at the puffy, white clouds.

"Fine, I won't wish to be older," she said. The world beneath her was spinning, and she, on top of it, was spinning, too. But it felt as if she were lying still. "I wouldn't have anyway. Probably."

Klara arranged herself beside her. She formed a matching T, the tips of her fingers grazing Emily's. "Okay, try this. Instead of wishing to get away from your mom, what if you wished for her to change?"

"To make her like me better, you mean?"

"She already likes you, dum-dum. She loves you. But . . . yeah."

Emily thought about it. Klara's suggestion made sense, but it seemed, somehow, like the wrong sort of wish. It wasn't up to Emily to change who her mother was.

"I don't know. Wouldn't that be an abuse of power?"

"So?"

"I could wish to have a better relationship with her," Emily mused. "That might work."

"Yes!" Klara said. She slapped the ground. "If things get better with your mom *now*, you wouldn't need to abandon me!"

"Oh, Klara. I'm not going to abandon you." She tilted her head and looked at the line of the forest. Trees stood tall and proud. Leaves rustled. The afternoon sun cast a buttery light over the infinite palette of browns and greens, and Emily's heart felt full.

Being alive was a gift.

Klara was a gift.

There were no such things as forbidden colors.

"If things were better between me and my mom, I could talk to her about visiting my dad," Emily reflected. "Maybe, eventually, I could even bring up the idea of going to live with him. Possibly."

"*Live* with him? But then I'd still miss you!" Klara wailed.

"And I'd miss you," Emily said. "And, odds are it

won't happen. But I wouldn't be *gone* gone. I'd come back to Willow Hill to see my mom, obviously. And you could visit me in California! We could have freshly squeezed orange juice whenever we wanted!"

Klara pouted.

"It's unlikely it'll happen," Emily repeated.

For a moment, Klara didn't speak. Then she sighed and said, "Oh, just ignore me. I'm being a baby."

She patted around and found Emily's hand again. "Of course I would visit you in California. Of course I'd see you when you came to see your mom in Willow Hill. You and me forever, right?"

Emily saw herself little again, driving away in the backseat of the car. "Forever and always."

"Good girl," Klara said. She squeezed Emily's hand so hard it hurt.

I wish I had a sister, or even a brother.

—TALLY STRIKER, AGE FOURTEEN

CHAPTER SEVENTEEN

~~~~~~~~

Ava

"Cousins?" Tally said to Ava incredulously. "You dragged me out here to announce, out of the blue, that we're *cousins*." She blew air out of her mouth. "Ava, you're adorable."

Her tone was sarcastic. Like Natasha and Darya, she was treating Ava as if she were a dumb little kid.

Ava *was* younger than Tally, and since Tally subscribed to the same logic her sisters did, Ava was more likely to be wrong. But in this case, she wasn't. She and Tally *were* cousins. She was almost absolutely sure.

The picture Tally had drawn was of her mother.

Tally's mother was named Emily.

Ava's mother, when she saw the picture, had known right away that it was Emily—*the* Emily, though older, who'd been her best friend when they were girls.

That meant the two Emilys were one and the same. Since Emily was Papa's little sister, that meant that Emily was Ava's aunt. It also meant that Ava's mother, Klara, was Tally's aunt.

Which meant.

They.

Were cousins. Ava and Tally.

Tally wasn't just Ava's cousin, either. She was Darya's and Natasha's as well.

Tally looked angrily at the sketch of her mom. She folded it up and shoved it into her jeans, her jaw tight.

"You're upset," said Ava. "You know why? Because you know everything I told you might be true."

"No, I'm *upset* because everything you're saying is ridiculous," Tally countered. Her voice was terse, which strengthened Ava's conviction. If Ava had told Tally that she was secretly an alien from another planet, Tally would have laughed. *Maybe* she'd have felt sorry for her. She wouldn't have gone all stony, building a fortress around herself for protection.

Ava knew in her bones that Tally's mother *was* Papa's sister and Mama's long-ago best friend. She could understand Tally's reluctance to believe it, however. After all, it sounded too good to be true.

Not just the part about being Ava's cousin. All of it.

Pauper to princess.

Orphan to heiress.

Girl shuttled from foster family to foster family only to discover—*gasp!*—that she had a big warm family of her own waiting just around the corner.

It was a huge, beautiful bubble, yes. It would be awful to reach out for such a bubble only to have someone pop it. But Ava wasn't going to pop it!

What piece of the puzzle had Ava left out? What would it take to get Tally to view the situation from a fresh perspective?

Of the three Blok sisters, Tally was closest to Darya. Could Darya be the way in?

"My sisters think I don't see them," she said, earning her another annoyed glance from Tally. "Especially Darya. Darya thinks I'm like, 'La la la, nothing's wrong with Darya,' but there *is* something wrong with her."

"Oh yeah? What?"

"Not wrong," Ava clarified. "Different. Darya changed after her Wishing Day, and you noticed it too. I know you did. You two had a fight right before her Wishing Day, and then afterward, you didn't talk to each other for like a week."

"More like two weeks," Tally muttered.

"Yes! Good!" Ava said. "I mean, not good, but . . ." She linked her arms behind her back, grasping her wrists and pulling hard. "Listen, sometimes the truth is hard to see. I get that."

"The truth?" Tally said. "There's no such thing as the truth."

"Maybe. Maybe not. Or maybe there are just different versions, and if you look at them the right way . . ."

"The pieces will magically fall into place?"

Ava reddened. "Maybe."

"See, that's the thing, Ava. You can't account for things using magic. Want to know why?"

"No, and I'm not—"

"You said magic is 'weird.' Your word. And by weird, you meant that magic doesn't have rules." Tally pushed her hand through her hair. "If magic doesn't have rules, you're basically saying it's a free-for-all. Can't explain something that doesn't fit your worldview? Blame it on magic! Problem solved!"

"I never said there weren't rules," Ava protested.

"You claim we're cousins. You claim there's *magic* involved. But you're conveniently skipping over something."

"What?"

Tally searched Ava's expression, and for a microsecond, Ava saw how vulnerable Tally was. Tally *did* want to be part of Ava's family, but there was more to her longing than that. Like everyone in the whole wide world, Tally wanted the gift of knowing who she was.

Then Tally's mask slipped back into place, flinty-eyed and stoic. "You can't use magic to explain things because magic isn't real."

Ava scowled. Magic was impossible to pin down, yes. That didn't mean it wasn't real.

Tally started walking. They were still on the path that would take them to the lake, but Ava took care not to point that out. Instead, she matched Tally's pace, or tried to. Tally was taller than Ava, and her stride was longer. Ava couldn't keep up without adding a jog here and there between steps.

"Last year, after Darya's Wishing Day, did she tell you any of her wishes?" Ava asked.

Tally didn't answer.

"Did she tell you her impossible wish?"

Tally snorted. "If a wish is *impossible*, then by definition . . ."

Yeah, yeah, yeah, Ava thought. "She didn't tell me,

215

either," she said, panting. "Not at first. I had to bug her and bug her and bug her."

"Fascinating," Tally said. Her arms swung at her sides, and her sneakers slapped the ground.

Sweat pooled at the back of Ava's neck as she took hop-skips to keep up. "Her wish was about your mom," she said, forcing the words out.

Pwoomf. Flesh smacked flesh as Tally came to a dead stop. Ava bounced backward, stumbled, and landed on her tailbone. "Ow!"

Tally stared down at her. "Darya made a wish about my mom?"

Ava extended her hand. "Are you going to help me up?"

"What do you mean she made a wish about my mom? What did she wish for?"

Ava sighed. She lowered her hand. "She wished to know the truth about Emily. All of it. Like, was there an actual Emily who lived in Willow Hill, even though no one remembers her? Did she grow up to be your mom? And, of course . . ."

"Go on."

Ava hated the next part. She would always hate the next part. "Well, if my mom *did* make Emily disappear . . . where did she disappear *to*?"

Tally jammed her hands in her pockets. She toed the ground of the footpath. "Not that I'm necessarily going to believe you, given that every word that comes out of your mouth is impossible," she finally said. "But what did Darya find out?"

This was the tricky part, as Darya's wish hadn't exactly been granted.

Yet.

"Ava? What's wrong, no answer?"

Ava slowly got to her feet, buying herself time. She could catch glimpses of the lake when the breeze blew certain tree branches certain ways, and the effect felt magical. Maybe it *was* magical, as if the world were giving her tiny windows—there and then gone—through which she could see her hoped-for future.

She reached a decision and continued walking forward. "Just come with me. You can see for yourself."

Tally complied, though grumpily. "If this is some wild goose chase . . . if this is some dumb 'Let's Play Pretend' game . . ."

Ava didn't rise to the bait. Instead, as they walked the last quarter of a mile to the lake, Ava doled out bits and pieces of her theory with Tally. She wanted to keep Tally engaged. She *needed* to keep Tally engaged. But if Ava said too much, or the wrong thing, Tally might throw her hands in the hair, spin on her heel, and stalk off.

That would be bad. Ava would be left without a spotter.

"My mom's version of the story," said Ava, "is that my mom and your mom—"

"*If* it's my mom."

"For the sake of argument, let's just assume—"

"Nothing. Let's assume nothing."

Ava had no bargaining power, so fine. She started over. "According to my mom, she and her best friend, *Emily*"—she gave Tally a loaded look—"were going to make their wishes together, because their Wishing Days fell on the same day."

Tally snorted. "Yeah, right."

"'Yeah, right,' what?" Ava said. "You know that a girl's Wishing Day is determined by when her birthday is, don't you?"

Tally looked wary.

"Well, when's your mom's birthday?"

"In March."

"March what?"

Tally looked alarmed. Had she been hoping Ava's face would fall? That Ava would admit that her mother's birthday *wasn't* in March?

"Just March," said Tally.

"Okay, well, my mom's birthday is March thirteenth," Ava said. She kept an eye on Tally, but Tally had regained control. She kept her face blank.

"Anyway, my mom and Emily were going to make their wishes together, at sunrise," Ava said. "But my mom made hers early."

"Why?"

"Because someone gave her bad advice," Ava said, oddly reluctant to throw the Bird Lady under the bus.

Then again, the Bird Lady had thrown Emily under the bus, so to speak.

"It was the Bird Lady," Ava admitted. "The Bird Lady told my mom to wish that she'd won that contest instead of your mom. Hold on . . . do you know about the contest?"

"Yes, I know about the contest," Tally said dangerously. Now, instead of drumming her fingers against her leg, she was clenching and unclenching her fist.

"And . . . so . . . she did," Ava said. "My mom wished that she was the one who'd won the contest. She did it to impress my dad, and the Bird Lady said it was fine, and even *your* mom—I mean, Emily—well, my mom said Emily didn't care all that much about the contest."

"Your mother wished that *she* had won the contest, even though someone else had already won," Tally said.

"Well, yes."

"And now you're telling me that the Emily who rightfully won the contest was my *mom*, whose name is also Emily."

"Um. Yes."

"Which means, if the Emilys are one and the same, that your mother erased my mother. That's what you're saying? That's what you believe?"

It sounded awful. It *was* awful, and Ava tried to let Tally have her anger. She tried not to think about the fact that every second they spent on this now was a second lost for other things. *Tick tock, tick tock.*

"When your mom left, when you were three or whatever, she walked away on her own two feet," Tally said. "When *my* mom left—and this *is* what you're telling me, right?—when she left, it was because of your mom's wish? As in . . . *poof*? Here one moment, gone the next? *My* mom did nothing wrong, and yet she's the one who disappeared?"

"Yes, but I'm going to bring her back," Ava declared. "And you're going to help."

"Like heck I am!"

They reached the lake. Tally stood beside her, radiating hostility. Gazing at the water, Ava explained what she was going to do.

Tally laughed, not in a nice way. "Yeah, that's a *great* plan. Sheesh, Ava."

"It might not be a great plan, but it's the only plan I've got," said Ava. "And you're the only one who can help me." She swiveled to regard Tally.

"Um, no. You could find a random stranger on the street to help you."

"Yeah, sure, a random stranger. Because that's how these things work."

"'These things'?" Tally barked a laugh. "There's no such thing as 'these things.'"

Ava leveled Tally with a stare. "Fine. You, Tally, are the only person with the incentive to help me." She gave each word the weight it deserved. "Don't you want your mom back?"

Tally made a sour expression.

Ava held her ground.

Tally scanned the lake, the path that circled the lake, and the vacant bench swing several yards from the lake. Then she looked at Ava. Then she looked at the lake again.

"Come on," Ava said. "It's really not that big of a deal." All Ava was asking was that Tally stick around while Ava was underwater, which would take two minutes, tops. If Ava didn't surface before the two-minute

221

mark—which she would, but just *if*—then Tally would pull her out. Two minutes was the longest most people could hold their breath before passing out, but even if Ava passed out—*which she wouldn't*—it wasn't as if she'd die.

Ava took a step forward. She took another step forward. She made her feet move—step, step, step; again, again, again—until she reached the water's edge, where she kicked off her sneakers and pulled off her socks.

Which she tucked neatly into her shoes, the left sock into the left shoe and the right sock into the right shoe.

"Ava," Tally protested unconvincingly.

Ava found herself more nervous than she'd anticipated. "I'm going!" she called to Tally over her shoulder. "I really am!"

Tally made an antsy huff that meant *do it or don't.* Ava didn't check, but she imagined Tally crossing her arms, maybe even tapping her toes.

Just relax, Ava almost called, but she stopped herself in time, not wanting to give Tally any reason to storm away.

Her own thoughts looped through her brain, and she got the chills.

I stopped myself in time, she silently repeated.

I stopped.
Myself.
In time.

She imagined a bug caught in amber, trapped in time forever. Except *not* trapped, and *not* forever. That was why Tally was here to babysit her.

Ava stepped into the lake, and the shock of the cold water jolted her into a state of hyperawareness. The sky was infinite, with a feathering of dove-white clouds. Diamonds of sunlight danced over the lake. A breeze lifted her hair and swooshed through the leaves of the nearby wax myrtles, making them stir.

Ava waded deeper in.

"Wait!" Tally called.

Ava turned around.

"Aren't you afraid?" Tally asked.

Ava lifted her eyebrows. Tally had gone on and on about how dumb Ava's plan was, but this was the first time she'd shown any anxiety for Ava's well-being.

"Yes," Ava answered honestly. "But I'm still going to do it."

Tally slipped off her shoes and socks and rolled up her jeans. She splashed through the water until she stood beside Ava.

Ava could hardly breathe. "Does this mean you'll

do it? You'll spot me?"

Tally folded her arms over her chest, and Ava was overcome by a swell of gratitude. She loved that people were always more textured than they first seemed. She loved that there were layers and layers and layers to everyone. She loved that through the murky water, she could see that Tally wore purple toenail polish.

"But you have to say your wishes out loud," Tally demanded. "I want to hear for myself that you're wishing for what you said you're going to wish for, and I want to hear the specifics and the clauses and whatever."

Ava blanched. Making her wishes out loud, in front of *Tally* . . .

"I don't think I can do that. It's too private."

"Ava? You're asking me to watch over you and make sure you don't die. I think you can."

"Omigosh, I'm *not* going to die. How many times do I have to tell you?"

"Right, because you'd pass out before that," Tally said. Using her Ava voice and sounding embarrassingly young, she said, "I'll be fine! Two minutes won't even give me brain damage!"

Ava blushed. "It's the truth."

"And here's another truth: If you want me to watch

over you, then I want to watch over you. Literally." She swished the water around them. "Right here, so I can keep my eyes on you."

"Here? It's, like, one foot deep. How would I stay underwater?"

Tally rolled her eyes. "I guess we can go out a little farther."

"Gee, thanks."

Tally spread her arms. "Hey . . ."

"No, no. Whatever." Ava chugged through the water: shin high, waist high, chest high. Tally kept pace with her. They were both nearly soaked by the time Tally grabbed Ava's arm.

"Here," she said.

Ava scratched her nose.

She curled her toes into the oozy mud at the bottom of the lake.

She let her body sway gently as the water rocked her like a baby.

"Do it or don't," Tally warned.

Ava took a breath and let it out. She was aware of the movement of her lungs, the expansion and contraction of her ribs. She nodded and pulled back her shoulders.

"First, my impossible wish," she said aloud. "For

my impossible wish, I wish for City Park Lake to be a membrane between different *whens*."

"Membrane?" Tally said.

Yes, membrane, Ava thought testily. Ava had thought about this and thought about this. She wasn't about to let Tally derail her.

"Just to be clear, I wish for City Park Lake to be a membrane between today and the past, when my mom was thirteen. Klara Blok. That's my mom. Although back then, she would have been Klara Kosrov. And only this part of the lake where I am right now, and only for me."

"Are you explaining this to the wish fairy?" Tally asked. "I mean, just to be clear."

"For the wish I can make come true myself, I wish to go underwater—right here, right now—and travel backward through time to the last day of the second month of my mom's thirteenth year."

"Sure, because that's totally within your grasp," Tally said. "I mean, obviously you can make that come true yourself."

"I can make myself dive underwater," Ava said defiantly. "*I* can do that. I can *choose* to do that. And I can choose to stay under for as long as I possibly can, to give the magic time to happen."

"*Ohhhhhh,*" Tally said. "Well, in *that* case. Why the last day of the second month?"

"So that I'll be there before my mom's Wishing Day. So I can get the lay of the land and figure out what to do on the *third* day of the third month after my mom's thirteenth birthday, since that's when she'll make her wishes."

"Of course. Yeah. Sure." Tally gave Ava a sarcastic thumbs-up.

"And for my third wish, the deepest wish of my most secret heart, I wish to return to this *when* once I've done what I need to do, and I wish to come back as me."

"That's two wishes rolled into one. Can you do that?"

"I just did, didn't I?" Ava shot back. She'd tried countless times to phrase it more concisely, but this was the best she'd come up with.

The breeze picked up, rippling the water and making Tally's hair fly crazily around her face. Ava's hair was in a ponytail, but even so, several of the shorter strands came free, lashing her cheeks and eyes. Goose bumps pricked all over her. Something powerful and wild coursed through her veins.

"My name is Ava Blok," she said under her breath.

"My name is Ava Blok."

A flock of songbirds erupted from a tree on the water's edge. Leaves fluttered, wings flashed, trills of music filled the air. *Starlings*, Ava thought, identifying them by their brilliant blue feathers. A murmuration of starlings; Papa had taught her that.

"Fascinating birds," he'd told her. "They mimic the sounds they hear around them—cell phones, car alarms, you name it. Once I met a guy who taught a starling to sing Mozart. Isn't that amazing?"

"Ava, Ava, Ava!" the starlings cried as they swooped above her in a loose oval.

"Ava?" Tally said, her eyes enormous. She stepped closer, reaching out.

Ava raised her arms above her head, pressing her elbows to her ears and bringing her hands together. She ducked her chin, bent her knees, and pushed. Water split at the touch of her fingertips, and the lake swallowed her whole.

CHAPTER EIGHTEEN

Ava

Ava held her breath for as long as she could. She dug through the thick mud at the bottom of the lake and found a root, or maybe a vine, to cling to so that she could keep from rising to the surface. Her feet, though. Her feet were like little helium-filled balloons. They floated up and up and up.

Get back down here, feet, she told herself, frog kicking to bring them back.

She thought of the endless tea parties she'd had with her sisters on the bottom of the public pool. On the count of three, Natasha, Darya, and Ava would suck in a big breath of air and sink to the bottom of the pool. They'd sit cross-legged on the bumpy concrete that always left nubbly spots on Ava's bathing suit bottom. They'd pump furiously with uplifted palms, pushing the water up so that they'd stay down.

Darya always won. Darya was always too stubborn to lose.

Ava swiveled her waist and fishtailed her legs in front of her, scissoring them until she was sitting crisscross applesauce. Yes, that was better. The root—or vine—was in front of her, her legs circling it and her hands gripping tight. The loose threads of her cutoffs fluttered like seaweed against her bare thighs.

A small wave rocked against her, and she swayed forward, then back. It was probably Tally. She was probably stepping closer, making sure she could still spot Ava.

Ava made an okay sign with her left thumb and forefinger and lifted her hand high over her shoulder.

Her lungs weren't bursting yet, but they were getting there. *Come on, come on*, she thought. *Happen!*

She closed her eyes. She tried as best she could to access any magic that might be waiting for her, but she felt nothing take hold of her. No whirlpool sucked her into another dimension. No gust of air formed a bubble around her and transported her to the "when" she hoped to arrive in.

Maybe the magic had happened without her feeling it? Maybe, when she opened her eyes, the lake water would be shot through with . . . rainbows, or points of shimmering light. Maybe there'd be a magical current, visible just to her. Or a wormhole! A wormhole in the water would totally fit her needs.

Please? she begged as she opened her eyes. *Please???*

Nothing.

Just Ava and the lake. The sweet, dear, boring lake she'd dived into.

A wave of disappointment crashed down on her—and then it was all over, because she couldn't hold her breath any longer. She let go of the root, pushed hard off the bottom of the lake, and emerged from the water.

Ava gasped in air. Oh, oxygen was good. She pressed her fingertips against her eyes, then swept one hand over her nose and pinched off any accidental snot. She sluiced water from her face and wrung out her ponytail. She regulated her breathing. She didn't turn around, because she didn't want to face Tally.

To Tally's credit, she didn't even clear her throat in an *I told you so* way. Tally didn't say a word—and yet Ava felt enormously ashamed that Tally had witnessed her failure.

"Fine," she said. Her sodden T-shirt clung to her body. She'd have to walk home sopping wet, which was great. Tally would be wet, too. They'd return to their respective houses, both dripping, and every so often Tally would shoot her accusatory looks.

"Seriously, go on and laugh," Ava said. She turned around. "You win. I lose." She furrowed her brow. "Tally?" She looked to the right. She looked to the left. "Tally? Omigosh, did you leave me?!"

Ava sloshed toward the shore. When the water was waist high, she pulled her shirt away from her body so that it didn't cling to her like a second skin. She flapped it a bit and squeezed what water she could from it.

"Tally!" she called. The water now reached her shins. She felt sticky, slimy, and dispirited. When she reached the pebble-dusted shore, she found that her shoes and socks were gone. Tally had stolen her socks and shoes, on top of everything else!

Really, Tally? she thought. *Really?!*

She picked her way toward the path encircling the lake, mocked by every rock she stepped on. Just past the thicket of trees and bushes that separated the lake from the trail, she stopped. Someone was there. Two someones. Two girls around Ava's age, sitting a couple of yards away on one of the rustic wooden swings.

232

Ava blushed so hard it hurt. How long had they been there? What had they seen?

She waited for the girls to do something, smirk at her or whatever, but the girls did nothing. They didn't seem to even see her, but please. No one could sit on a swing in front of a lake and not notice when someone emerged from said lake like the creature from the black lagoon, gasping and making *pfff* noises and shucking water from her hair.

She studied them, worried that any minute they'd lift their heads and laugh at her. They didn't. They were just really involved in whatever they were talking about. Really *really* involved, their heads bowed and their shoulders touching.

Ava shivered, a full-body twitchy shiver that came out of nowhere. The weather had changed, she realized. The sky was still blue and the sun shone cheerfully, but the temperature had dropped. An hour ago, Ava had been sweating as she tried to keep up with Tally. Now the air was cool on her skin. She needed to move.

She wiped each muddy foot across the opposing shin to clean them off. She stepped out from the trees and gave up, saying, "I'm weird, I know. It's a long story."

The girls kept murmuring in low voices about

whatever it was that was oh-so-important. As mortified as Ava was, their nonreaction felt like a slap.

"Seriously?" she said. She walked all the way to them and she waved her arms like a roadside traveler beckoning for help.

"Hello-ooo!" she called. When they did nothing, Ava got right up in their faces, her humiliation bubbling over into near tears. "What you're doing is mean," she said, looking from one girl to the other. "It's called ghosting. You're ghosting me out."

She snapped her fingers in front of the girl on her left, who wore a Dr Pepper shirt. Mama used to like Dr Pepper. These days, she said it hurt her stomach.

Dr Pepper girl blinked and glanced Ava's way with a puzzled expression, but almost immediately turned back to her friend. Ava huffed and clapped her hands directly in front of the other girl, who had light brown hair and looked familiar, though Ava couldn't think from where.

"I know I'm being silly," said the familiar-looking girl. She looked down at her lap and not at Ava at all. "But it'll be over soon one way or the other, right?"

"Don't think of it as being over, Emily," Dr Pepper girl said. Ava's heart stopped. *Emily?* "Think of it as a new beginning!"

The familiar-looking girl—Emily—groaned and

put her head on Dr Pepper girl's shoulder. "I wish I didn't worry, believe me."

"*Wish,*" Dr Pepper girl said. "Ha!"

Emily rolled her eyes. "Omigosh, Klara. You honestly don't have a worry in the world, do you?"

Ava grew light-headed. She'd felt as if her heart stopped when she learned Emily's name. Now, hearing Emily say Mama's name—*Klara*—her heart stopped all over again. When it started back up, it pumped her blood the wrong way through her veins. She felt as if she were in a dream, watching a play unfold before her—and she was part of the play herself, even if the other players didn't know it.

The two girls sitting before her on the swing weren't ghosting her after all. She'd ghosted herself, when she made her Wishing Day wishes. She, Ava, was the ghost.

CHAPTER NINETEEN

Ava

She pushed her hands hard against her temples. She was a *ghost* and as a ghost, she had to find the Bird Lady!

Only, she *had* no hands. She realized that only after looking down at her body and seeing that she had . . . well . . . no body. She'd seemed to have shed her physical form as she sloshed through the lake. She'd squeezed the water from her shirt, after all.

Her now nonexistent shirt.

She was still herself—still Ava—but in spirit form. *Whoa*, she thought. It was possible and impossible at the same time, and the contradiction lifted her spirits.

Spirits! Ha!

Oh, good heavens, Ava had the same goofy sense of humor as the girl on the swing who'd said, "Wish! Ha!"

If she wanted that girl—Klara—to grow up to be her mother, she needed to get going. Same for the other girl, Emily. This Emily *was* the Emily who would grow up to be Tally's mother, Ava was sure of it. Ava could see the resemblance between thirteen-year-old Emily and the Emily from the picture Tally had drawn.

As for the initial flicker of familiarity Ava had experienced?

Oh. Riiiight. Emily, at age thirteen, resembled Ava at thirteen. Or Ava resembled her?

That's why Grandma Rose had called her Emily, and Papa, too. She'd given them just enough of a nudge to almost remember the real Emily.

The Bird Lady, she reminded herself, and with a scattering of light and a whoosh of wind, there the Bird Lady was, in front of Ava.

Or, wait. The lake, the grassy lawn, the bench swing. Klara and Emily. They were gone, replaced by the shadowy forest that bordered the park. The Bird Lady hadn't come to Ava; Ava had gone to the Bird Lady.

"Oh, phew," Ava said as she landed—if that was the right word—in front of her. The Bird Lady didn't immediately see her, though. The Bird Lady stood half-hidden by a large maple tree, peering out from behind it and watching something avidly. She held her hand to her mouth, and her eyes sparkled with delight. She looked as if she were enjoying something delicious.

Ava looked over her shoulder. Yes, yes, she didn't have a shoulder, but it felt as if she did, and so she decided to go with it. Perhaps some mainframes were too ingrained to shed.

What she saw made her gasp, though she made no sound. *The Bird Lady was spying on Emily and Klara!*

"My pet, my girl, my angel," the Bird Lady murmured. She clapped and bounced on her toes. "Sweet Klara! I'm here for you, pet. I'm here!"

She turned and scurried into the forest, and Ava hurried after her.

"Hey!" she said. "*Hey!* We have a plan, remember?"

Only, crud. Ava and the Bird Lady made their plan *in the future*. At the present, Ava was in the past. Past, present, future . . .

Omigosh, Ava thought. *Too much!*

The Bird Lady reached the oak tree where her hideout was. The great oak, covered in Blue Moon wisteria.

The Bird Lady found one particular knobby root and ducked into the hollow, and like a whisper, Ava was there as well.

She watched as the Bird Lady scribbled words on a scrap of paper, her tongue poking out of the corner of her mouth. *Klara Kosrov*, she wrote on the top.

"How to help, how to help," she muttered. She tapped her lip with the pen, then scribbled some more.

"No, no, *no*," said Ava. She tried to maneuver in front of the Bird Lady. *The Bird Lady wrote through her.*

Yick.

"This is not the plan," Ava said. She tried to take the pen from the Bird Lady. Her efforts were wisps of air against metal and ink. "Why can't you hear me? Aren't you supposed to be able to hear me? You hear the thoughts of thirteen-year-old girls, remember?"

The Bird Lady hummed and fussed, writing the words *Nate* and *Olympiad* and *a mother with three daughters.*

Ava would have sworn if swearing was something she did. Since she didn't, she stomped around and kicked at the soil. Her actions yielded no results.

Okay, breathe, she told herself. *What am I forgetting?*

Oh! The Bird Lady could hear the *thoughts* of thirteen-year-olds! Was that the cause of the mix-up?

Pushing on her words with fierce intensity, she thought, *Look at me. See me. Stop writing stuff down about my mom!*

The Bird Lady hummed and rolled up the scrap of paper. She dug through a crate of glass soda bottles and pulled out one that was a murky shade of green.

"Not one of your stupid scrolls!" Ava cried. The idea of her mother's dreams being rolled up and stuffed into a bottle made her feel nearly hysterical. She tried pulling the Bird Lady's hair, but found no purchase.

You are supposed to HEAR me! she yell-thought with all her might. *You hear thirteen-year-old girls, you dumb old Bird Lady!*

Then Ava remembered . . . and the air was sucked from her lungs, the hope from her heart.

Ava wasn't Ava, yet. She was, well, the potential of Ava. The Bird Lady couldn't look into Ava's eyes and see Ava's soul, because Ava hadn't been born yet, which meant that Ava didn't *have* eyes yet, not eyes that the Bird Lady could see. Ava's soul was still her soul—Ava was convinced of that—but the Bird Lady couldn't access it, so to speak.

"Two days, two days," the Bird Lady trilled as she wedged the last bit of the scroll into the tight glass bottle neck. "Two days until your Wishing Day, dear Klara."

Ava freaked out. *Two* days? But Ava had wished to go back in time with the goal of arriving three days before Mama's Wishing Day. Three days, not two!

Everything was wrong! What was it Mama had said? Mama and the Bird Lady had both said it, that Willow Hill's magic was "fluky."

But where did that leave Ava? Communicating with the Bird Lady was a wash, and Ava had even less time to fix things than she'd anticipated.

Mama, she thought. *I'm trying. Really, I am!*

Longing washed over her: for Mama, for thirteen-year-old Klara and thirteen-year-old Emily, for wholeness and rightness and love.

She reeled as once again came a scattering of light and a whoosh of wind. This time, she arrived in a bedroom. A girl's bedroom, with a pale blue comforter on the bed and an assortment of teddy bears propped against the pillows. Hold on—she recognized one of the teddy bears! He was in better condition than she'd ever seen it, but it was Johnny, all right. Brown button eyes, soft plush fur . . . Johnny the teddy bear, who belonged to Ava now.

Well, not in *this* now. But he would. Ava, in the present, had slept with Johnny all through her childhood.

He'd been Mama's, Papa had told her. Ava felt comforted when she held him.

If Johnny was here, that meant . . .

Yes. Klara. Her one-day mother was sitting at a small desk, doodling in a notebook. Ava peered over her shoulder, and her lungs squeezed together when she saw the hearts Mama was drawing over and over, filling each with a variation of *Klara + Nate*.

"Mama?" Ava said tentatively.

Klara kept doodling.

"Mama, it's me."

Still nothing.

"Klara," Ava tried.

Klara's back stiffened, but only for a moment. She shook her head.

Ava moved closer. She touched—or imagined touching—Mama's arm, and goose pimples popped up all over Klara's skin. Klara looked at her arm and inhaled sharply.

"This is real," Ava said. "You're okay. You're not . . . going crazy or anything."

Klara rubbed at both arms, the way someone does when they're trying to warm up. She was unnerved, Ava could tell, but she still couldn't *hear* Ava. Ava felt like crying. The Bird Lady had neither seen nor heard her, and now it seemed that Mama—Klara—couldn't either. What was the point of her wishes if she couldn't communicate with her mother?

Working yourself into a frenzy won't help, Ava told herself. *This is a puzzle. You have to figure it out. So figure it out!*

With Aunt Elena, she'd had the sense, for the briefest of flashes, that she and Aunt Elena had connected telepathically. It was when Aunt Elena was trying to remember who could confirm her story about Emily being real. It turned out to be the Bird Lady, and it had been Ava who helped Aunt Elena find the answer in her mind. How had she managed it then?

Through focus, concentration, and single-mindedness of purpose, like the articles she'd read had suggested. She'd imagined sending energy from her mind to find energy from Elena's mind—*and it had worked.*

She'd done the same thing with Klara, and it hadn't! What was different???

With Aunt Elena, Ava had told her aunt about telepathy. She'd asked Aunt Elena to try it with her as an experiment, and Aunt Elena had agreed. They'd both been on the same page. Also, they'd both been strongly connected already, because they'd been talking about the same thing and wanting the same thing.

How could Ava connect with Klara when Ava had no connection with Klara, not Klara as a thirteen-year-old?

But she's your mom, Ava told herself. *That. Is. A. Huge. Connection. And fine, maybe she's not your mom yet, but she* will *be.*

Ava gave a jolt. The letter Mama left for Ava before walking away from their family for eight and a half years! Ava had been disappointed in the letter when she first read it—and she'd been disappointed on her second, third, and all other future readings, too. Mama had told Natasha and Darya the good stuff, that was how it seemed to Ava, while to Ava, she'd basically said, "I'm weary now, my darling. Your sisters will fill you in."

There'd been one other part, though. At the time, Ava hadn't thought it was important. Maybe it wasn't.

But maybe it was.

Mama, in her letter, had told Ava a story illustrating how stubborn Ava was. She'd told her how for an entire year—the year leading up to Mama's departure, in fact—Ava as a toddler had insisted that Mama read one book and one book only to her at bedtime every night.

The book was called Love You Forever, Mama had

written. *Do you remember? It was about a mother and a son, and every night, the mother sang the son a song that went like this: "I'll love you forever, I'll like you for always, as long as I'm living, my baby you'll be." It was a sweet book, and a sweet song, though part of the song always rankled me. You, Ava, will be my Ava even after I'm done living. For that matter, before! You, Ava, will be my baby forever. Please hear me. Please believe me.*

In the book, the boy grew older and older, and when the boy was a man, there'd been a funny illustration of the mother creeping in through his window and rocking him in her lap even though he was huge. Then, at the end . . . and it made Ava feel teary even now . . . the tables had turned. The mother was old and feeble, and the *son* had held *her* in his lap. The son held his dying mother in his lap and sang the familiar song, changing the last line to "As long as I'm living, my mother you'll be."

Ava sang the song now. Her voice made no sound, but she sang it with all her heart. She imagined her mother as a baby, her mother as a teenager, her mother as her mother. She imagined herself in her mother's embrace. She imagined Klara in her own invisible embrace.

"As long as you're living, my mother you'll be," she sang.

For too many minutes, nothing happened. But one of the articles she'd read at Rocky's Diner said that ghosts—or energy untethered to a physical body—*could* communicate with living beings, so she didn't give up.

"As long as I'm living, your baby I'll be," she sang, changing the final line for her own purposes.

It's me, Mama, she thought as she sang, texturing the words with that one-day truth. She pushed on that thought with all her might. Again and again, she imagined energy flying from her to her mother . . . and it happened! A door edging open, the same way it had happened with Aunt Elena!

Brilliant light . . .

Tiny wings . . .

Confusion, and Mama, and Ava as a baby.

Then, like two layers of a picture sliding together to form a single image, their spirits merged.

Ava swelled with exaltation. *Mama, it's me!*

Thirteen-year-old Klara put her hand to her face. She said, "Omigosh, I'm going crazy."

You're not, don't worry! But you might, if you don't listen to what I say. Molecules buzzed and hummed. *Can you hear me, Mama? I mean, Klara?*

For real? Nod if you can!

Klara tilted her head, rested her ear against her cupped palm, and did that jostling thing with her hand as if she were trying to get water out.

That was as good as nodding, Ava decided.

Except bubbles of fear clogged Klara's blood. Ava tasted metal. The bubbles were so dense and airless they could drown a girl. Could Ava drown within her own future mother?

Klara's heart raced, and Ava experienced it as if her own heart was racing. Klara breathed shallowly. Ava breathed shallowly.

Whoa, Ava thought.

"Whoa," Klara said, and Ava felt the weight of Klara's emotions. It was a richer tapestry than she'd initially realized. Anger and fear, yes, but also sadness. The way Klara let her body slump told Ava how helpless she felt.

But you're not, Ava told her. *I'm here. I'm here to help.*

"Who are you?!" Klara demanded.

Don't you know? Didn't you listen? I'm Ava.

"Ava," Klara said flatly.

Yeah. I'm, well . . . I'm your daughter.

Klara's pulse skyrocketed.

In the future! I'm from the future! Ava rapidly

explained. *Years from now, you'll have three daughters: Natasha, Darya, and me. And guess what? You do marry Nate Blok!*

Klara didn't try to boot Ava out. Instead, she allowed their connection to strengthen. Ava knew there was no science to confirm it, but she sensed that they were connected as deeply as they were because everything Ava was saying was true. Ava *was* Klara's future daughter. Klara was flabbergasted at Ava's presence, so Ava repeated to Klara her own mantra. *It's okay. Sometimes impossible situations call for impossible solutions, that's all.*

"Yeah, sure, that's all," Klara muttered. "And what did you mean, I grow up and marry . . . Nate?"

A flicker show of impressions raced through Ava: A photograph of Ava's family when Ava was three and their family was whole. Then Mama, depressed. Mama abandoning not just Ava, but also her sisters, Vera and Elena; her other two daughters, Natasha, Darya; and, of course, her husband.

Nate.

Emily's brother.

Ava's one-day Papa.

Klara knuckled her eyes. She said, "Okay, I didn't get all that. I'm not sure I want to."

No problem, Ava said. *That's why I'm here, to make sure none of that happens. To make sure Emily doesn't—*

"Doesn't what?" Klara pulled her bare feet onto her chair and hugged her knees. "When you think about Emily, it's like a black hole or something. Everything goes shadowy."

Ava's thought went skittering. *Don't tell her about Emily being erased,* she cautioned herself. *Not yet!*

"Erased?!" Klara said. "Did you just say *erased*?"

Ava tried to close off her brain—except, why? This was the reason she was here, wasn't it?

"Everyone loves Emily!" Klara went on. "No one would 'erase' her, ever!"

No one but you, Ava thought, and it was out, despite her effort to ease into it more gently.

Ava, formless though she was, clapped her hand over her mouth. If not acting like a person who still had a body was hard, not thinking the thoughts she wanted to banish was even more difficult.

Oh, just go ahead and do it, she told herself. She relayed to Klara the future that might be, and Klara bolted out of her room and into the bathroom, where she dropped in front of the toilet and threw up.

Oh, Ava thought. *Oops . . . ?*

Klara retched again, and then once more, even though her stomach was empty. She grabbed some toilet paper and swiped at her mouth. Then she stood, unsteadily, and cupped handfuls of water into her mouth, rinsed, and spit. She stared at herself in the mirror.

"Are you really . . . ?" she asked.

I am, Ava said. She felt a wrenching twist of sympathy for this girl, her one-day mother, who hadn't yet done anything. Not anything bad, that is. *And . . . I'm sorry.*

"But *why*—" Klara gave a hard shake of her head. She *did* believe Ava. Ava could feel it. She might not understand, but she believed.

Someone knocked on the bathroom door. "Klara?" said a small voice. "Are you all right?"

Klara startled. "Um . . . I'm fine!" she called. "Upset stomach. Better now!" Peering again at her sallow complexion, she whispered, "I just won't make my wishes at all, then."

Ava snapped to attention, knowing that wasn't the answer. The wishes mattered. The magic mattered.

Go to Emily, Ava thought.

Klara felt a rush of relief. Ava felt it with her, a stripe of sunlight in a windowless room. Emily was

Klara's best friend. She needed her best friend at a time like this.

First thing in the morning, Ava prompted. *Now, bed.*

Klara nodded. She dried her hands on the hand towel and returned to her room, passing a very young, very cute Aunt Elena wearing a comical expression of concern.

Snuggled beneath her covers, Klara shivered and turned off her bedside lamp. She and Ava slept.

CHAPTER TWENTY

Emily, age thirteen

"Wait. What?" Emily said. It was the day before Klara's and her Wishing Day. They'd planned everything out, down to the last detail. Then Klara had arrived at Emily's house before school started, pale and agitated and shifting her weight from one foot to another. She'd dragged Emily to Emily's bedroom and shut the door, jabbering about stuff that made no sense.

The most disturbing part? Klara wasn't Klara. Or, she was, but she wasn't the Klara Emily was accustomed to. She was Klara Plus, kind of.

"We have to stay together," Klara said. "The Bird

Lady—she isn't the batty nice lady I thought she was."
She screwed up her face. "Or . . . no . . . that's not right.
She's . . ." Klara's gaze grew unfocused. "I missed that.
What?"

Emily rubbed her arms. She and Klara were the
only ones there, and yet Klara looked for all the world
as if she were talking to someone else. Someone in her
head. Worse, Emily could almost *feel* someone else in
Klara's head.

Except that was crazy, obviously.

Maybe she's got a stomachache, Emily thought.

"She *is* nice," Klara said emphatically. She focused
again on Emily. "The Bird Lady's nice, but she's confused. She wants to make things better, which is good.
Only she doesn't yet know that what she's planning to
do will make things *worse*, which is bad."

"I don't understand," Emily said, not for the first
time. She'd tried several times since Klara had arrived
to push on Klara's thoughts in order to gain some sort
of clarity, any clarity, about what had happened to her
friend. Normally, she stayed out of Klara's head, but
she'd decided that this was a special case. Klara was
acting *so* strange.

Emily couldn't, though.

She couldn't push her way in.

Something (or someone?) was blocking her.

Shivers ran up her spine. She rubbed her arms more vigorously, trying to warm up.

"Emily," said Klara abruptly. She stared at Emily with wide eyes. "This is going to sound really out there . . . but do you think maybe you have, like, psychic powers?"

Emily paled.

"Please don't get scared," Klara said. "Ava just—I mean *I* just . . . I just have this feeling that you do."

"Do *you* have psychic powers?" Emily said, hearing her pulse in her head. If Klara had a gift like she did, how had she failed to notice for all these months and even years?

"No! I wish!" Klara paused, again adopting her listening face. "Or, maybe I do, but . . . they're on loan."

"You're scaring me, Klara."

"For what it's worth, I was scared, too. I threw up, even."

"You threw up? When?"

"Last night, when, um, it first happened."

"When *what* happened? Klara, tell me what's going on!"

Klara pushed her hand through her hair, which was wild and unbrushed. "It's going to sound impossible. It is impossible. But—"

Klara seemed to fight an internal war with herself. She closed her eyes and groaned, then stared at Emily with resignation. "My daughter is here. From the future. It has to do with her wishes."

Emily had no words.

"She says not to feel bad," Klara went on. "She says that the Bird Lady couldn't sense her, either. Maybe because she's not, you know, real yet?"

"Not real *yet*," repeated Emily. "Your daughter from the future?"

"I know. I *know*. Her name's Ava—"

"She has a name?!"

"Well . . . yeah! And supposedly, Ava reminds people of you, so you shouldn't be mean to her."

Emily held out her hands, palms up.

Klara puffed out a breath of air. "She thinks she's blocking you from, like, reading my mind, so she's going to get out of the way for a bit. I don't know how, so don't ask."

"I wouldn't dream of it," murmured Emily.

"Oh, God, Emily. There's so much you need to know!" Klara cried. "It's life or death, literally. So just . . . help yourself?"

And then it was as if a veil was lifted from Klara's thoughts. Emily felt a jolt. Time seemed suspended for several long, mind-bending moments.

Then time started up again, and Emily heard an insistent buzzing. She tried three times to shake the buzzing out of her ear before realizing that the buzzing was real. She uncoiled herself from her spot on her bed and strode to her window, cracking it open to free a honeybee that was bashing itself repeatedly against the pane.

"So . . . do you know now?" Klara said. "All of it?"

Emily returned to her bed and perched next to Klara. She prodded, but Klara's mind was closed again.

"She—Ava—is back in?" Emily said.

Klara nodded.

"Right," Emily said. She felt foggy from the information dump she'd just undergone. It was as if she'd read a book in its entirety, but had yet to absorb its contents—and there was *so much* to absorb. "Can you give me a minute?"

Klara nodded again: up, down, up, down.

Emily wondered if she was as pale as Klara was. She felt the lurching terror of free fall, imagining the future Ava came to warn them of, and was at once resolute.

"I agree with . . . Ava," she said at last. It was odd, talking about someone who was both there and not there, but it had to be done. "We can't not make your wishes at all. We can't not make our wishes out of fear." She cocked her head at Klara. "You'd seriously wish that you won the contest instead of me?"

"No! Never!" Klara's face distorted, and Emily wondered if Ava, and the truth, sat like stones within her. "I don't know—and, to be fair, the contest results haven't even been announced."

"They're announcing the winner this morning," Emily mused. "And tonight, according to Ava, the Bird Lady was going to come to your house? Throw rocks at your window and persuade you to wish you'd won instead?"

"Not tonight. Early, early tomorrow morning, right after midnight. But Emily, I haven't made that wish, and I won't. All right?"

Emily considered this.

"You're my best friend," pleaded Klara.

Emily sighed. "And you're mine. And you're right, or the Bird Lady's right, that I don't care all *that* much about being the winner. But if it happens—"

"Which it will, which I've been predicting all along!"

"Well, if it does, that would feel pretty good. *I* would feel pretty good."

"As you should! I don't know what I was thinking!" She thumped her forehead with the heel of her palm. "Except I *don't* think that, and I won't."

"My mom didn't make her Wishing Day wishes," Emily mused.

"And did it hurt her? No."

"I'm not sure that's true. If she *had* made her wishes, maybe she'd believe in magic. If she believed in magic . . ."

Klara caught on. "Oh. Maybe she'd understand you better." She frowned. "So . . . ?"

"I think my mom feels safer in a world without magic. I think it made her world flatter, though. All her life, she's done her best to scrub her life clean of surprise, but where has that gotten her?"

Klara didn't answer.

"If we don't make our wishes—or if you *don't*, Klara, because I'm going to no matter what . . ." Emily studied her friend. "You'd never choose to give up your eyesight, would you? Or your hearing, or your sense of smell?"

"All right, all right. I hear what you're saying. I'll . . . I'll make my wishes. I'll make the exact wishes I've been planning on making, and I won't change them at all."

Emily made a face.

"What?"

"You're forgetting about Ava," said Emily.

"What about her?"

"She's here with you—with us—because she wished to be. She used her Wishing Day wishes on us. That's pretty cool."

Klara blushed. "I guess it is. I hadn't thought of it that way." She gave a tremulous smile. "She said impossible situations call for impossible solutions."

Emily saw pride in Klara's eyes, and for an instant, she could see the wonderful mother Klara would one day be.

"But Ava needs to get back to her own present, doesn't she? So, you might need to revise your wishes after all," Emily said. "I'm not telling you what to wish for. I don't have a clue about any of this, believe me." She chose her words carefully. "Just, if our wishes are supposed to come from a pure place, an honest place . . ."

Emily saw a glimpse of another time, another possible outcome. The magic that might have taken Emily and *erased* her . . . Emily caught just the flickering reflection of yet another truth, one that cut her to the core. Her mother already didn't see her, not really.

After years and years of living unseen, might Emily have disappeared regardless? Might the magic be telling Emily to see this truth clearly now?

"Things are different than they were yesterday," she said. "We know things that we didn't know before, and we can't unknow them."

"Changing what I wish for because *I* choose to is different from letting the Bird Lady convince me to," Klara said. "I get it."

"There's more," Emily said, and her heart almost cracked as she shared her revelation with Klara. When she made her request, Klara shook her head vehemently.

"No!" she protested. "How is that different from . . . you know?!"

"Because it is."

A tear squeezed from Klara's eye. Then another. Her chin wobbled, and she took a ragged breath. She glanced away from Emily, which told Emily that Klara would honor her request. This small good-bye was a preview of what was to come.

They talked about how to proceed. Klara wondered aloud if she should spend the night at Emily's to avoid the Bird Lady, or if the Bird Lady would find her at Emily's just as easily?

"And what am I supposed to say to her if she does find me?" Klara said. "Everything feels precarious."

"Everything *is* precarious," Emily said. "I don't think you should interact with the Bird Lady at all. You or me. We'll ignore her if she tries to talk to us."

At first, Klara agreed. But then she changed her tune. She told Emily that they couldn't just avoid the Bird Lady, as much as they might want to.

"I don't understand," Emily said. "Are you saying this, or Ava?"

"Ava—but she's right."

Emily arched her eyebrows.

"We can't avoid the Bird Lady because of all the other girls," Klara said hollowly. "The girls to come." She wrapped her arms around her ribs. "We have to tell her to stop messing around with other people's wishes."

"After school, then," Emily said reluctantly. "We'll get it over with, and we'll still have time to spare."

"Not much," Klara said.

"No. But enough."

CHAPTER TWENTY-ONE

Ava

Ava was disappointed to find that going through a school day with Klara was almost as tedious as going through a school day on her own, except for the assembly in which the principal announced the winner of the Academic Olympiad.

"Let's hear it for Emily Blok!" he heralded, launching a loud, long roar of applause. When Emily returned to her seat beside Klara, Klara gave her a fierce hug. She was happy for Emily. Ava felt that happiness in every one of Klara's cells.

Emily's mother, who had been invited to the school for the assembly, sought Emily out after the students were dismissed. Ava, through Klara's eyes, saw a small, prim woman whose eyes darted back and forth. Ava saw a small, prim woman who one day would be her grandma Rose, who one day would be small and prim in the care center where Future Ava would go to visit her.

Emily's mother, who one day would be Grandma Rose, hugged Emily and loudly exclaimed how proud she was of her. Then, lowering her voice, "For heaven's sake, why didn't you wear that nice blouse I ironed for you this morning?"

Emily's expression went from happy and open to wary and cautious. *Ava* wanted to hug Emily now, hug her for real, the way Klara had. "Mom, kids don't really wear . . ." She blinked. "That blouse is too fancy for school."

"But you won an award! You were called to the front of the entire auditorium!"

"Because of the contest, Mom. Not because of how I dress."

Her mother made a sound of exasperation. "It was your chance to shine. I don't understand you, Emily. I really don't."

The principal came over and clapped Emily on the back. He held out his hand to shake Emily's mother's hand, and she simpered.

"You've got a fine daughter, Mrs. Blok," he said.

"Yes, oh, yes, we're all very proud of her," she said. "It's hard, as you might imagine, to be a single mother with such a"—she gave a strained smile—"*unique* child, but an honor like this . . ."

The principal regarded her quizzically.

"Well," Emily's mom concluded. "It's good motivation, right, Emily? Hopefully affirmation from your peers will encourage you to continue to work on fitting in."

The principal opened his mouth, then closed it. Uncomfortably, he congratulated Emily once more and excused himself. Emily's mother followed his lead, her heels clicking down the hall as she hurried off.

"Sorry for that," Emily told Klara.

"What? No," Klara said. She took Emily's chin in her hand. "Hey. *Hey.* You *do* shine, always, and it's not your job to apologize for your mom. If she can't see how awesome you are, that's her problem, not yours."

Yay, Mom! Ava cheered, making Klara's insides go funny. Ava quickly amended her message. *I mean Klara. Yay, Klara!*

So weird, Klara thought. *This whole world is so frickin' weird.*

But there's nothing wrong with weird . . . right? Ava asked.

Klara slung her arm around Emily and said, "C'mon, weirdo. Time to go receive more affirmation from your peers."

Emily laughed weakly.

Ava glowed.

The rest of the day was full of teachers and lectures and classroom discipline. Today, of all days, it was a chunk of time to endure and little else.

When the last bell chimed, Ava helped Klara find the Bird Lady's oak tree hideout. Emily followed quietly behind.

At first, the Bird Lady was thrilled to see them, but she got skittish when they confronted her about her plans to talk Klara into changing her wish. Ava could tell that the Bird Lady felt guilty, as well she should. Klara and Emily explained about Ava and the future and how badly everything would turn out if the Bird Lady interfered.

The Bird Lady pulled herself up tight and denied it all. "I have no idea what you're talking about," she said frostily. "You're making up stories about me just to be cruel, and I won't listen. I refuse."

Ava spoke to Klara in her mind, and Klara reached for the glass bottle that held the scroll with Klara's name on it.

"No, no, these are my things," the Bird Lady said,

spreading her arms and blocking the way. "You're not going to steal from an old lady, are you?"

"How old *are* you?" Klara said, but Ava hadn't really meant for her to. It slipped out of Ava's consciousness and into Klara's, that's all.

"None of your business," the Bird Lady said.

"Ma'am?" Emily said.

The Bird Lady jutted out her lower lip. "No. Whatever you're selling, I don't want it. Nothing you can say will change my mind."

Now was the time, Ava realized. Ava told Klara the Bird Lady's secret, and when Klara gasped, Ava felt the gasp resonate through her. She felt so connected to Klara—her one-day mother. She *was* so connected. Was this what it was like to be in the womb? Would she really be reborn as her own self one day?

Yes, you will, Klara told her fiercely. To the Bird Lady, out loud, she said, "We're not here to steal from you. We're not here to blame you, either. And we're not making all this up. You know that what we told you is true; I can see it in your eyes."

The Bird Lady hemmed and hawed. She said, "Well, and what's the harm? Maybe I was going to come to you tonight. *Maybe* I was. Wouldn't have been the catastrophe you're making it out to be."

"Except it would have," Klara said. "That's why we're here. I'm safe now, and Emily's safe, but you can't meddle with the wishes of anyone else, ever."

The Bird Lady's face fell. "I . . . I just want to help. All I've ever wanted is to help, and perhaps be appreciated a bit. That's all." She blinked and grew stubborn. "And so I will. You can't tell me not to."

"Would you want to even if you knew you weren't helping? Even if you knew you were making things worse?" Klara pressed.

The Bird Lady's eyes looked shifty.

Klara lowered her voice. Gently, she said, "When your mother died, she whispered something into your ear."

"No!" exclaimed the Bird Lady. Red blotches bloomed on her face. "How do you know that? No one knows that! I was the only one with her!"

"She said, 'You are perfect just the way you are,' and those were the last words she spoke." As Klara spoke the words, Klara—and Ava—were flooded with compassion. "*You* told my daughter that, or you will. Time is . . . fluky. Jumpy. But you told my one-day daughter, and you told her for this very reason: so that you would believe me and listen to me and stop meddling."

267

The Bird Lady attempted to bluster her way around the truth, but gave up. Fat tears spilled out of her eyes. "I thought if I helped people, they'd be grateful. That maybe they'd come visit me sometimes." In a voice barely above a whisper, she said, "All I've ever wanted is for people to like me."

Emily reached out to touch her. "We *do* like you."

"And we'll come visit you," Klara added. "We promise. Just, no more meddling with other girls' wishes, ever." She regarded the Bird Lady sternly. "Can you do that?"

The Bird Lady asked Klara if she would tell her again about her mother's last words to her, and Ava knew it wasn't because she doubted Klara's story. It was for the comfort of being reminded of her mother's love.

Klara indulged her. After repeating the story, she said, "It sounds like your mom loved you a lot."

"She told me to 'be my own girl,'" the Bird Lady said wistfully. "I suppose I lost track of that, didn't I?"

Klara hitched her shoulders. "It's okay. We all mess up."

"It's late," Emily said, tugging gently on Klara's sleeve. "We should go home for dinner."

Ava nudged Klara to ask the Bird Lady something else before they left.

Klara listened. She said, "Huh." Then, to the Bird Lady, she asked, "What's your name? Your real name?"

The Bird Lady eyed them.

"If we're going to be your friends, shouldn't we know?" Klara pressed.

The Bird Lady cocked her head from side to side. She stilled herself and swallowed. "It's Grace," she said with dignity.

"Grace," said Klara.

"It's beautiful," said Emily. "Bye, Grace."

"Bye, Grace," Klara echoed. "We'll see you soon. I promise."

Klara and Emily turned to leave.

"Wait!" cried the Bird Lady—or rather, Grace. "Wait please, darlings. Just for a moment?"

Klara and Emily shared a glance. They turned around.

"I do have one piece of advice for each of you, but it's not meddling, I promise." She looked at Emily and said, "Emily, be your own girl." She looked at Klara. "Klara, be your own girl."

"We will," said Emily and Klara together.

I wish for a happy ending.

—NATASHA BLOK, AGE FOURTEEN

CHAPTER TWENTY-TWO

Emily, age thirteen

At sunrise the next morning, at the old willow tree on top of the hill the town was named for, Emily flung her arms around Klara and hugged her tight.

"It's not good-bye," she said. "It's see you soon. Right?" She laughed a tear-clogged laugh and took a step back. They held on to each other, each girl's hands on the other girl's shoulders.

"Absolutely," Klara said shakily.

"You're still worried."

"Well, yeah. I mean, we're making all of this up as we go along, when people's lives are at stake. Like Ava's."

"It is what it is," Emily said.

"I know, but . . . I keep thinking about how much courage it took, what she did. She's thirteen, the same as us. Can you imagine doing what she did? Leaping into such a huge unknown?"

Emily almost could. After all, she hoped she'd be leaping into the unknown herself.

"She did it for you," Emily said.

"She did it for us," Klara said. Then, softer, "Thank you, Ava."

"Yes," Emily said. "Thank you, Ava." She looked deeply into Klara's eyes, blocking out everything else. No filters, no posturing, no shying away from the terrifying question of what it meant to be alive in this world. She lost herself in Klara's dark pupils, stepping purposefully into the abyss. *Ava? Ava, are you there?*

A shimmer. That was all, and that was enough. Emily put her hand to her mouth, reeling from the wondrous bigness of it.

Klara squeezed Emily's shoulders and let go. "Okay," she said shakily. "You first."

Emily lifted her chin. There was magic in the air, most definitely. In a voice as clear as a bell, she spoke.

"For my impossible wish, I wish to have a better relationship with my mother. For the wish I can make come true myself, I wish to stay best friends with Klara forever." Her voice tried to escape her, but she didn't let it. "And for the deepest wish of my secret heart . . ." She trailed off and spoke the last bit from her heart. (((((Daddy.)))))

She blinked at Klara, light-headed.

"Good job," Klara said. "You did it."

I did, didn't I? Emily thought. She said, "Thanks. It's your turn now."

"I'm going to go all the way to the willow," Klara said. "Will you come with me?"

"Of course." Emily ducked under the willow's graceful canopy and held up a section of fronds. Klara joined her, and they stood side-by-side by the willow's great trunk. The willow had been alive long before either of them had been born and would be alive long after they were gone.

The early morning sun cut through the branches, dappling Emily and Klara with spots of impossible colors that, nonetheless, were possible. Emily stretched out her arms, her soul soaring. She lifted her face, stretched her arms wide, and soaked it in.

"Well . . . ," Klara said.

Emily's heart beat faster. She knew in general what Klara would be wishing for, but not the exact specifics.

A breeze made the branches sway, and Klara placed her hand on the willow's trunk. Now the breeze whipped through the branches, and Klara's hair blew crazily about her head. Emily's hair was tossed and tangled, too. The air prickled with what felt like electricity, but Emily suspected it was a force far wilder.

"Um, I'm going to close my eyes," Klara said. "I have to, because I can't watch. But you can do whatever you want."

"Got it," Emily said, moved by the tears Klara wiped away.

Klara scrunched her eyes ferociously. "First, my impossible wish. I wish for impossible things to become possible, every so often."

Emily smiled, because *yes*, Klara had gotten it just right. Wasn't that what Ava had told Klara, that impossible situations call for impossible solutions?

"My second wish is the wish I can make true myself," Klara said shakily. "I wish that Emily and I grow up to be good mothers, and that our daughters grow up to be good mothers, and that their daughters

276

grow up to be good mothers."

As Klara spoke, Emily felt a change in the air pressure, as if there was a ripple in the atmosphere. She was hit by a flood of images, and she knew she was seeing in her mind what Klara was seeing in hers.

A girl, probably thirteen years old, coughing and spluttering as she emerged from a lake.

Beside her was the Bird Lady. Grace! She looked the same as she had when Emily saw her yesterday, save for her outfit. In the vision in Emily's head (*was* it a vision of the future? It *felt* like a vision of the future), Grace wore a sequined pantsuit. *Wow.*

"There, there," Emily heard her say, patting the drenched girl's back.

"Hey! Gentle!" someone else said. It was a girl with long, dark hair like Klara's. She was older than Klara and Emily. Did Klara, in the future, have three daughters, just as she'd hoped? Was this Klara's oldest daughter?

The older girl stood chest-deep in the water with Grace. Beside her were two other girls, one of whom said, "She's fine, Natasha. You're fine, Ava. Right?"

This girl laughed and did a victory dance in the water, her curly auburn hair gleaming in the light of the setting sun.

"Darya!" said the girl named Natasha, squealing and drawing back. "You're splashing me!"

The third girl in Emily's vision had her back toward Emily, her hands planted on her hips. Something about her made Emily's heart leap, and Emily wanted to see her face. She suddenly and desperately wanted to see the third girl's face, but before she did, the vision faded. Everything was obscured, as if by snow or static or a zillion mini-marshmallows raining from the sky, and Emily was back beneath the willow tree with Klara.

Goose bumps rose on Emily's arms, and again she felt the rightness of Klara's wish. To be a good mother implied growing up and *being* a mother, which underlined Klara's desire for Ava to be safe. Also, good mothers were raised by good parents, which included mothers *and* fathers, as well as guardians of any sort. And since Klara included Emily in her wish . . .

Was this her way of honoring Emily's request? Would Klara's wish lend strength to Emily's wishes, about both her mother *and* father?

Daddy, whispered eight-year-old Emily within Emily's thirteen-year-old soul, and for an instant, Emily understood: All time *was* all time. It neither changed nor lent itself to explanation. It simply was.

She sensed her body rising into the air. She looked

down at her hands, flexing her fingers. Each finger floated apart, cells scattering like birdseed.

She wiggled her feet—only she no longer had feet.

She smelled ocean spray and the tang of citrus. She saw a man in a sunlit kitchen, holding a phone to his ear.

"Yes, we just got back from the airport," he said. "I'll put her on the phone." The man covered the speaker. "Emily? Emily! Your mom wants to talk to you!" He spoke again into the phone. "Tell Nate hi for me, and that I'm working on his plane ticket for summer break." His voice broke. "And Rose? Thank you."

Then that vision faded, and Emily saw Klara, small and far away.

Or maybe Emily was small and far away?

She heard Klara's voice, just barely.

"And for my last wish, the deepest wish of my secret heart," her best friend said, and her words were bubbles, balloons, sweetly buzzing honeybees. "I wish for us to remember. To remember just enough, but not too—"

Not too what? thought Emily. *Just enough, but not . . . too much? Was that what Klara said?*

Emily's thoughts became bees.

They hummed and buzzed.

"Klara?" Emily tried to say.

Emily's thoughts, her cells, her dreams, her soul—they were one, and they were all. They transported her to a land of milk and honey.

And orange juice.

I wish for mysteries: infinite, beautiful, and magical.

—GRACE

PROLOGUE: EUGOLORP

[decorative flourish]

"**O**kay, open your eyes!" Natasha cried, moving her hands from Ava's face.

Nine-year-old Ava blinked. She sat cross-legged on the picnic blanket Mama had thrown onto the grass for the kids, her elbows on her knees and her hair tickling her back. Her hair was *long* now, really and truly long. Longer, even, than her oldest sister's hair, because last month Natasha had asked if she could get a fancy haircut for her sixth-grade graduation, and Mama had said yes.

Immediately after her fancy haircut, Natasha had burst into tears and implored Mama to glue her cut-off hair back on.

"Oh, baby," Mama had said, tucking the strands of Natasha's pixie cut behind her ears. "The world doesn't work that way, I'm afraid. We can't turn back time. But it's just hair. It'll grow back."

And that was true. It would. But until then, *ha*! Until then, *Ava* got to be the Blok sister with the longest hair!

She smiled, remembering the time she'd gotten gum stuck in her hair. Mama had suggested cutting the gum out, maybe cutting all of Ava's hair to chin length, but when Ava had protested, Papa had swooped in and saved the day. He'd smeared peanut butter on the gum, and in the process smeared peanut butter over her whole scalp, practically—gloopy and sticky and awesome.

Her sisters had thought it was hilarious, especially Darya, who was the middle sister of the three Blok girls. Darya and Natasha begged Ava to hold her big, gooey peanut-butter head still and pretend to be a squirrel feeder, so they could catch a squirrel. Ava refused. They begged her to hold still while they threw cotton balls at her, to see who could get the most to stick to her head. She refused. They threw cotton balls at her regardless, until her head was a massive, fluffy cotton-ball explosion. She was a walking Q-tip, and secretly, she loved it.

And eventually, Papa did get the gum out, as well as the cotton balls. Win-win for everyone.

"Ava," she heard. "Ava!"

She returned to reality to see Darya's face a foot away from her own.

"Oh," said Ava. "Hi!"

Darya rolled her eyes. To the others, she said, "Omigosh. Ava went off with the fairies again, people."

"Because fairies are awesome," Ava retorted. "Except—oh yeah. You wouldn't know, would you?"

Darya was ten and Natasha was eleven, but even so, the two of them were in the same grade at school, both one grade higher than Ava. While Natasha was all about studying and getting good grades, Darya's world revolved around makeup, fashion, and saying things like "omigosh" and "dude, that's so savage."

On top of that, Darya *pretended* not to believe in fairies. Not just fairies, but any sort of magic, period. Which meant that honestly, Ava had no choice but to make fun of her.

Darya stuck her tongue out.

Ava batted her eyelashes and smiled.

"Well?" said Tally, who sat on her knees, her fingers curled in anticipation. Tally was the reason they played the "Ava and the Fairies" game. Tally loved the idea of fairies and unicorns and every sort of magic there was.

Ava tapped her chin and gazed at the clouds. "Hmm," she said. "Hmm, hmm, hmm."

Darya groaned.

Natasha said, *"Ava."*

But drawing it out was part of the tradition, as Natasha and Darya knew. They were just playing their roles—although Ava wondered how much longer Darya would agree to be part of it before deciding it was babyish.

Natasha already thought it was babyish, Ava suspected. But Natasha was the kind of girl who liked making others happy, and Tally and her mom only visited once a year. Tally's dad came even less often, because he was a physicist and very busy with that and other grown-up stuff. He was Italian and had an accent and wore his hair in a man-bun.

Uncle Fio, Aunt Emily, and Tally lived in California, which to Ava sounded exotic. They wanted to move to Willow Hill, though, and Ava could totally understand why. Willow Hill *wasn't* exotic. The small, tightly knit town of Willow Hill was the opposite of exotic, and it would be hard for Aunt Emily, who was an art curator, to find work here.

But Ava wouldn't want to live anywhere else, ever.

She suddenly felt woozy with love. She loved Mama and Papa, and she loved their small, cozy house. She loved Aunt Emily, who was Papa's little sister, and she loved her cousin, Tally. She even loved slightly scary Uncle Fio. She loved her aunts on Mama's side, too: Aunt Vera and Aunt Elena, who lived in Willow Hill and visited often. They were here now, chatting and laughing with Mama, Papa, and Aunt Emily.

The girls' auntie Grace was here, too. Auntie Grace wasn't related to Ava and the others, not technically. But she'd been part of Ava's life since the day Ava was born. She was the best, kookiest Auntie Grace ever. She shared meals with Ava and her family once or twice a week, and she baked the most delicious brownies. She was rarely serious, and she told fabulous stories. Ava, her sisters, and Tally all adored her.

Ava knew with every fiber of her being how blessed she was. Even as a nine-year-old, she knew that her certainty was a blessing, too.

Ava exhaled, blowing the air out with a *pfffft* sound. She locked eyes with Tally, who was flushed with expectation. She cleared her mind and let things happen as they would . . . and there it was, the hum of energy Ava and Tally were sometimes able to call forth.

Natasha and Darya didn't know about this part.

This part was just for Ava and Tally, and it was why the two of them would go on believing in magic long after Natasha and Darya moved on to other things. Or so Ava hoped.

"The windowsill of the farthest window to the right, on the porch," Ava said clearly.

Tally rose to her feet and sprinted off. Darya gave Ava a half smirk, but when Natasha hopped up and followed Tally, Darya dashed after them both.

"Hey, wait up!" she cried. "Wait for me!"

Ava grinned. She lay down on the quilt, extending her legs and resting the back of her head on her overlapping palms. A honeybee flew in a lazy circle above her, and Ava said, "*Hola*, bee. What do you see? Do you see me, bee?"

Bees had compound eyes; Ava had learned that in science. Each eye had thousands of lenses, which blew Ava's mind.

Did that mean that the honeybee saw thousands of Avas? Or did it see thousands of different parts of Ava, parts that could be fit together like a puzzle to form a full picture of who Ava was?

She floated off for a bit, her thoughts like rising bubbles. When the bubbles popped, her thoughts joined the fabric of the universe. *She* joined the fabric of the universe.

Feet pounded the ground, and Ava propped herself up on her elbows. "Well?"

"We found something!" cried Tally, rosy-cheeked and shining. She flopped onto the quilt and held out her hand, her fingers cupped in a loose fist.

Natasha and Darya dropped down on either side of her. They glanced at Ava over Tally's head, including her in what they thought was a shared conspiracy. Sometimes it was. Sometimes Ava had one of her sisters hide a stone under a sofa cushion, or asked them to place an especially lovely feather in the kitchen cupboard. Once, she persuaded Natasha to stick a dandelion in Aunt Vera's bun.

Other times, Ava didn't need their help. If Darya chose to assume that Natasha had planted the treasure, however, that was fine. Same for Natasha when Natasha suspected Darya of sneakily acting on Ava's orders. Ava let her sisters believe what they wanted to believe.

"Show me," she said to Tally.

Tally smiled and opened her hand to reveal four mini-marshmallows.

"Nice!" Ava said. "I didn't know if they'd be marshmallows or acorns, but I was hoping for marshmallows!"

Tally passed them out, and each girl popped hers

into her mouth. Magic, soft and sweet, melted on their tongues.

The honeybee made one last pass above their heads.

Bye for now, bee, Ava thought. *See you later.*

The bee hovered in front of her, frozen in time for just a moment before buzzing away.

I wish for children to play beneath my branches and nap in the shade of my leaves. I wish to know their stories: what they've done and what they will do. I wish to see the whole world unfold before them.

—THE WILLOW TREE

ACKNOWLEDGMENTS

Ooo baby, this book was a tough one! One of my top writing challenges, for sure. Why? Because it's the third in a trilogy. Trilogies are always hard. Also, because I ended *The Forgetting Spell*, book number two in the Wishing Day trilogy, with a fantastic cliff-hanger ending. Yay me! Only, then it came time to write *The Backward Season*, which meant answering the momentous questions left dangling at the end of *The Forgetting Spell*, and . . .

I got it wrong. Many, many times. And each time, my amazing editor, Claudia Gabel, gently told me that I'd gotten it wrong. My bonus amazing editor, Alex

Arnold, concurred. Each time. Many, many times. So many times.

We brainstormed, we talked things out, we plugged away and plugged away again. Claudia and Alex refused to settle for "almost, but not quite." They refused to let me—or themselves—settle for less than our very best. Even though it was REALLY, REALLY HARD. So hard! And finally . . . we got it right. We told Ava's story the way it needed to be told. Is it perfect? No. But it is the result of blood, sweat, and tears, and I sure am proud of it. The process made me a better writer, which is to say that Claudia and Alex made me a better writer. So, Claudia and Alex? THANK YOU. I acknowledge y'all and acknowledge y'all, with gratitude and love!

Also, tremendous thanks to the entire Harper-Collins team, especially the two sweet Stephanies: Stephanie Boyar, for championing these books so tirelessly, and Stephanie Guerdan, for being so frickin' tolerant of my (many!) requests to change things one last time. Stephanie G? You are a goddess to me.

Thanks to Anica Mrose Rissi, of course, for being awesome. Thanks to my agent, Barry Goldblatt, for believing in me more than—cough, cough—sales figures occasionally warrant. Thanks to Bob, the best water-cooler buddy ever, and a special thanks to Ermengarde Lockhart, Sara Zarr, and Tara Altebrando, for cheering me on in our Decemberists Club. And a bonus thanks to Ms. Lockhart, as well as the fabulous Sarah Mlynowski, for chatting with me almost every day and ALWAYS making me smile. ☺

As always, huge thanks to my friends and family. Y'all are the magic in my world.

And Randy, my sweet, strong, brilliant husband. You will always be my wish come true.

Read them all!

"Heart! Humor! Sisterhood! Magic! Myracle's new book has it all."
—Sarah Mlynowski, *New York Times* bestselling author of the
Whatever After series and coauthor of *Upside-Down Magic*

 KATHERINE TEGEN BOOKS
An Imprint of HarperCollins*Publishers*

www.harpercollinschildrens.com